PRAISE FOR THE NOVE

The Children of Pithiviers

"Kohler weaves an intricate and endlessly surprising tale of betrayal. Her vivid, sensual writing and her heart-breaking account of the fate of two of the many children imprisoned in the camps of Vichy France make this a beautiful and important book."

— MARGOT LIVESEY, author of *Banishing Verona*
and *Eva Moves the Furniture*

"Kohler's slim volume holds in its easy grasp the liveliness and the corruption, the yearning and the evil that run just below our civilized skins."

— *Time Out* New York

Cracks

"A disturbing note-perfect novel. Dissection of evil has rarely been so extravagantly executed."

— *San Francisco Chronicle*

"Delicious and dark . . . with sensuous, shimmering imagery, [Kohler] tells a story of teenage tribalism, awash with dreamy eroticism. Kohler's language is poetic and elegant and brilliantly visual. . . . Hauntingly good."

— *Elle*

"Written with a real atmospheric nostalgia that conjures up the wildness of the veld, and the passion and drama of adolescence . . . a sustained piece of storytelling, and a peculiarly satisfying novel."

— *Times Literary Supplement*

SHEILA KOHLER is the author of five novels, including *The House on R Street, The Perfect Place* (available in Other Press paperback edition), *Cracks,* and *The Children of Pithiviers* (forthcoming from Other Press Paperbacks). Her novel *Cracks* was chosen by New York *Newsday* and *Library Journal* as one of the best books of 1999. She has also published three collections of short stories. A native of South Africa, she makes her home in New York City and teaches at Bennington College in Vermont.

ALSO BY SHEILA KOHLER

NOVELS

The Perfect Place
The House on R Street
Cracks
The Children of Pithiviers

SHORT STORIES

Miracles in America
One Girl
Stories from Another World

Sheila Kohler

CROSSWAYS

— a novel —

For
Barbara
with all good
wishes
Sheila Kohler

Other Press · New York

10 9 8 7 6 5 4 3 2 1

Library of Congress Cataloging-in-Publication Data

Kohler, Sheila.
  Crossways / by Sheila Kohler.
     p. cm.
  ISBN 1-59051-209-X (pbk. : alk. paper) 1. Married women–Crimes against–Fiction. 2. Traffic accident investigation–Fiction. 3. Johannesburg (South Africa)–Fiction. 4. Hospital patients–Fiction. 5. Sisters–Death–Fiction. I. Title.
  PR9369.3.K64C76 2005
  823'.914–dc22

                                                        2005017631

ACKNOWLEDGMENTS

I would like to express my gratitude:

to the Yaddo foundation, where much of the character of Louis came to me, thanks to the great gift of long hours of silence and solitude;

to the Dorothy and Lewis B. Cullman Center and the New York Public Library Fellows of 2003, where many of the revisions were made;

to my fellow teachers and the students at Bennington College for their support and encouragement;

to those generous friends who read this book in various shapes and forms;

and particularly, Frances Kiernan for careful editing and wise advice;

Amy Hempel for the great gift of her friendship;

Marnie Mueller for support, encouragement, and thoughtful suggestions;

my agent, Robin Straus, who has been there from the start;

Charles Shields for his help with the Zulu language;

Credo Mutwa for his courage and wisdom and the spirit that gave us the wonderful "Indaba my children" and guided me through parts of this book;

to my editor and publishers: Raymond Smith and Joyce Carol Oates, for their example, support, and generosity;

to my darling daughters, Brett, Cybele, and particularly Sasha Troyan, who read this manuscript many times;

and, once again, to my husband for his selfless love and generosity and his respect for the English sentence.

"Sometimes these selves would converse in the void;
and then madness was very near, as I believe it would be near
the man who could see things through the veils at once of two
customs, two educations, two environments."

—*The Seven Pillars of Wisdom* by T. E. Lawrence

For my sister's children
Vaughn, Lisa, Simone, Alexia, Claire, and Winnie

PART ONE

I

S HE ARRIVES AT CROSSWAYS in the spring, only this time, it is
death that brings her back. She looks along the driveway
to see if John is coming. She remembers him striding down the
dusty path under the alley of jacarandas in his khaki uniform
and swinging open the gate, standing there with his high,
narrow head tilted back slightly, as if listening, and one arm
raised with the Zulu greeting, when she and her sister would
come home from boarding school for the holidays. But there is
no one there to greet her today.

Kate is sweating in her tight black suit. Her lips are dry and
cracked, and there is a sick ache behind her eyes from the long
voyage out and the visit to the mortuary. Her head spins. A fly
buzzes against the back windshield.

Break-ins and car-jackings and rapes have become more
frequent recently, particularly out there, her sister Marion has
written. Despite the draconian efforts of the government, crime
remains rife, and rebellion simmers beneath the smooth surface
of the divided society. It is the late seventies, and the white
government still clings to its lost cause. Kate thinks of her

lover's last words at the airport in Paris. "Ten days. Don't stay out there more than ten days. Please."

Now she nods her head and tells the driver to advance. He steps slowly out into the killing light, looks around warily, yanks at his khaki trousers, and struggles with the white gate. He pushes it open, climbs back into the car, and drives cautiously under the arch of fine leaves and the branches where Marion and she perched as children.

No cars wait in the shadows of the open garages, neither her sister's silver Mercedes nor her mother's Jaguar. The windows of the big house are shuttered and silent. No one, apparently, has bothered to remain at home to greet Kate at this hot hour of the early afternoon. Even her sister's dog, Rosie, seems to have disappeared.

Kate thinks she will have to grow accustomed to this silence. She wonders if her mother feels that the wrong child has been killed, that it should have been herself, the younger, more troublesome sister, or perhaps her mother can no longer allow herself to love any child after the great grief of losing one of them.

She imagines the family out for a consolatory drive in the Jaguar: her aunt Dottie in her flowered hat and kid gloves, sitting in the front seat beside the driver with the dog panting at her feet, and her mother, a little pink in the face, fanning herself with a knitting pattern in the back, the children sitting solemnly at her side.

At the thought of her sister's three children, all under seven years old, Kate's throat closes, and she feels she cannot breathe. She has come out here for the birth of each of them and held them in her arms. She remembers Mark as a plump, dreamy boy with curly brown hair. Lydia was the one who resembled Kate the most, as she was as a little girl, skinny and fierce and willful, with hectic pink cheeks and tight pigtails tied with big, bright bows like butterflies flying down her back. Marion referred to her last child, the white-haired baby, as "the icing on the cake."

Despite the children, Kate has not wanted to come back here even now, though she has had no choice, of course. When her mother called in the night with the news, Kate was lying in her lover's arms.

She thinks of him, a long-haired French poet, who was born in Germany but has lived all his life in France. Rene has a rather antique appearance with his Trotsky glasses and an earring in one ear and on formal occasions a velvet bow tie in a midnight blue.

She met him in the late sixties, when she introduced and translated his first book of poems, from the French, a book she called, "Permutations." It took her almost a year to complete, translating slowly, painstakingly moving words back and forth, saying them out loud to herself in the bath.

She remembers how he held her against his thin, trembling body as he kissed her good-bye.

Now Kate sees smoke coming from the servants' quarters, which are at some distance from the house, but no one emerges to welcome her when she steps out of the taxi. She wonders if anyone has told John of her coming, if he is resting in his room. This is the dead hour of the afternoon, when the servants, who rise early and work late, take their rest.

So she takes her black bag herself from the driver, who lifts his hand in a kind of salute, mutters the Zulu farewell, and leaves fast, glad to get away, she suspects.

She steps back and stares at the creeper-covered edifice. She and her sister's children are the ones remaining now to inherit this vast house, Crossways, in the suburbs of Johannesburg.

She listens to the sound of the water falling over the brick wall and into the pool, and of the cicadas hissing in the stillness of the afternoon.

She thinks of her father, who left his family and came up from the coast and was lucky enough to acquire fourteen acres of high veld from a mining magnate down on his luck, for a thousand pounds. It was he who had this house built by a deaf architect of some renown. She contemplates the green Dutch front door and the tubs of pink and blue hydrangeas on either side. Then she walks around to the back like a tinker or a thief.

Tired as she is, she lingers in the small patch of shade, blinking in the brutal glare. The feathery leaves of the jacarandas cast faint shadows.

She carries her suitcase in one hand, unable to prevent her handbag strap from dropping from her shoulder and sliding down. She breathes deeply, deliberately, taking in the familiar smell of this place, the smell of stale heat and memories, rising from the earth.

All of this was once as familiar, as much part of her, as the features of her face. When their father died, her mother said she wanted to move into a flat, that the big house would be too much for her on her own. Kate's sister asked what would happen to their ridgeback dogs? She said she would run away, that she would rather die than leave the house. So, they had stayed, the aunt and eventually the uncle moving in with them.

Kate wonders if her brother-in-law, Louis, will ever be able to return here. She watches a dry leaf, driven about by a random gust, just as she chased after Marion, in their identical pastel smocks, their Dutch caps, their slippery button-up shoes, playing hide-and-seek.

She looks at the lawn rising and falling away toward the bamboo and the long grasses where they played their secret games, and the flat earth stretching out to the blue hills. She thinks of how the first adventurers must have come upon this scene, unaware of what shimmered beneath the dun grass of the high veld, the rich vein of ore, which would be fought over so fiercely, and the bloodshed which would ensue.

She sees the house as a ghostly red ship, destined to hover forever between jacaranda masts.

She tries the back door, which was always left open while her sister was alive, but finds it locked tight. She looks around uneasily and plunges her gloved fingers into the leaves of the creeper, feeling for the hole in the wall where the key was always kept, disturbing the dust, and, perhaps, the rats. Her father had always maintained there were rats in the orange, trumpet-shaped flowers, which covered the walls of the house, though she has yet to see one.

Kate remembers the mouse which Marion had rescued. It had escaped its cage and found its way into Kate's towel. She lifted it to her face, and the mouse scurried down her neck and into her blouse. Kate screamed and fell down, cracking her head on the black and white tile. She was always fainting or pretending to faint, as though her head were too far from her heart and inaccessible to the necessary blood. She would float down from her pew at communion, or during the dressmaker's pinning of her skirt, or on a crowded bus, coming down easy like the light mauve flowers of the jacaranda trees.

Fumbling, she finds the key in the hole near the polished brass handle on the green door and grasps the key case eagerly to her chest, rubbing it between finger and thumb, her mother's old key case with its cream leather worn gray, never replaced over all these years. She turns the key in the lock, drops her suitcase just inside the door, and stumbles, half-blind, into the dead quiet and the muted light of the shuttered house. She sees again the old *kist* and the grandfather clock with the golden angels' trumpets held aloft, and a shiver passes up her spine, the same sensation she has when reading a familiar and lovely line of poetry, a pause of recognition and mystery.

She stands before the mirror over the mahogany chest and removes her new black garments: the soft leather gloves, feathered hat, smart linen jacket now stained with sweat, and tight patent-leather pumps. The enclosed silence of the old house assaults her. There are no roses in the silver pitcher in the entrance hall to welcome her, and even the pitcher itself is gone. Is there then no one left here to call her name, to hold her against her heart?

Now she pads in dark stockings slowly up the stairs, smelling the familiar air, too long enclosed. A servant has left the windows clamped shut to keep out the heat, she presumes.

She crosses the landing with a sensation of nausea, remembering the spoonful of thick castor oil which they were made to swallow after breakfast for their health. She wanders down the corridor and into the large room which was once their nursery. The walls are no longer that pale, bilious green, and the blackboard is gone. The two wooden beds and the bedside cupboards with their chamber pots, for her sister, and her, have been replaced by three white lacquered ones, but there are the familiar teddy bears and dolls, heaped in piles on the pillows, as there were on their beds, long ago. Her heart beats like a drum. Through the bay window where they often sat, the sun comes in aslant. She looks out at the lawn below and sees in her mind the two children in the garden, holding hands and watching out for the *Tokolosh*.

Every room in the big house and every flower, bush, and tree in the garden had its own character and had to be treated specially. Everything had to be handled carefully and according to certain rules in order to avoid the dangers that lurked in them and that might tear them away, divide them from each other, and destroy them.

She goes back along the corridor, carrying her shoes. She pads into the master bedroom and stands still, catching her breath and leaning against the wall. Her sister's bedroom, which was once her mother's, in the east wing, has been left much as it was when her mother used it, with the dressing table, the three-way mirror, the old-fashioned mauve velvet curtains, the pelmets, and the faded silk bedspread. She traverses the screened sleeping porch and the spacious dressing room, goes into the bathroom, and turns on the taps. The blue-green stain in the enamel under them is still there.

She strips off the rest of her clothes fast and lets them fall to the floor. She stands naked by the bath, piling her hair up on her head. She gives her black underwear a kick, not so much out of anger as from the effort required to keep doing one thing after another.

She was not with her sister when she died. She did not hold her in her arms or tell her good-bye. She had not seen her for months. How could she have anticipated such a sudden, violent death?

In warm water she throws her head back and stretches out her legs, as Marion and she did so often, sometimes together, in this big tub with its old-fashioned feet, before Kate left to go to Paris to study French at the Sorbonne. Kate left shortly after she had finished boarding school in the early sixties, not long after Sharpeville. She came home for short visits to her sister only every two or three years, though they had written regularly.

Lying in the water, Kate sees her sister as she saw her at the mortuary where she had asked to see the body.

The man had worn a waistcoat despite the heat and an eye-patch. He looked at her for a moment, with his good eye, hesitating. "Are you sure you want to do this?" he asked, a little hoarsely. He had a cold. "I don't advise it," he added and blew his nose.

She is not sure why she insisted. She is not usually good at insisting. Weighing things so carefully in balance, she often has difficulty making up her mind. She sees both sides of every question. Conflicting images quarrel in her mind like the ones of this beautiful country, which she both loves and hates. She has difficulty saying she believes this or that. She is not sure she knows what she believes, an uncertainty she feels helps her in her translations, if not in her life, enabling her to enter the minds of the different authors whose work she translates.

Perhaps she asked to see her sister's body because she could not believe she was dead, or perhaps she wanted to be near her, as she had been as a child.

They had wheeled the body into the adjacent room behind glass, so that Kate could see her. She walked over and stood with her hands on the glass, her breath misting it. The body was completely wrapped, even the neck. Only her small flower-face was visible, the lovely skin gray, the little chin thrust forward slightly, as though seeking the sun, propped up so that Kate could see her.

Instead of forgetting her past, Kate is now remembering more and more, as though her own life is slipping from her, and she is turning toward the dead.

She sits up in the bath and turns on the taps but hears in her imagination her sister's voice, calling her in the sound of cascading water.

She rises, the tips of her fingers wrinkled, her hands shaking. She steps out of the water and dries herself with her sister's big thick towel, hung over the warming pipes and smelling of her perfume. She wraps herself in Marion's pink silk gown, which still hangs behind the door, and ties the belt tightly around her waist.

She wanders into the dressing room, trying to ignore the ache behind her eyes. She surveys her sister's husband's elegant linen suits, Louis's Gucci shoes with the tassels, Hermes ties, the shirts in all the colors of the rainbow, all presents from his wife, Kate surmises. Louis, like their father, is not known for extravagance. On a high shelf she catches a glimpse of his old-fashioned, bulging doctor's bag. She reaches up and pulls it down, and opens it, fingering the stethoscope, the tongue-depressor, and the reflex hammer.

She opens and shuts the drawers filled with her sister's clothes: her pastel-colored kid gloves with the seed-pearl buttons all the way to the elbows, lying there in placid piles, the neat nylon underwear, the embroidered Swiss hand-kerchiefs, and the folded scarves. She opens another closet and finds their mother's gin bottle with all the *tiekies*, still hidden behind countless pairs of delicate shoes, and in the corner, pushed against the wall in its plastic cover, her sister's old-fashioned, dark-blue net dress with the sequined bodice, which she wore as a girl, but had always kept, because she loved it best. Kate unzips the bag, puts her hands into the layers of net, lifts it to her face, and smells the odor of dust and flowers and lost dreams.

She goes into the bedroom and sits at her sister's dressing table with its three-way mirror and cream organdy skirt. She brushes and combs her long brown hair with her sister's silver brush-and-comb set and ties it back from her face.

She picks up the initialed mirror and turns it over. A jagged line runs across the surface of the glass. "A broken mirror brings seven years' bad luck," she hears her mother say. When was it broken? She remembers a letter from her sister, telling of a burglary some months back. Some of the silver was stolen. Her sister had wept over the lovely English pitcher, which had always been filled with roses of different colors and kept on the console in the hall.

She walks down the stairs and goes through the dark pantry, which still smells of oranges, and into the big kitchen, looking for something to eat and drink.

Nothing has changed in the kitchen either: the big pullout bins for flour and *mielie* meal, the well-scrubbed pine table, the spiky climbing plants in the windowsill, the fat, old-fashioned yellowed refrigerator. Even the old coal fire in the courtyard, where the servants once cooked their food, is still there.

She opens the refrigerator door and stares in disappointment at the almost empty shelves, realizing she has eaten nothing on the plane and hardly anything for days, since learning of her sister's death. There is nothing but a half-eaten jar of pickles, a wrinkled apple, and a carton of milk.

"Surely someone could have left me some food!" she says aloud and drinks from the carton, wiping the milk from her upper lip with the back of her hand. Her head feels transparent and light, and her hands are shaking. She is rocking again, her knees buckling with grief. She leans against the whitewashed wall.

She goes back into the sunken lounge, sits down on the piano stool before the baby grand, and runs her hands with their short, rounded nails—her sister's hands—over the yellowed keys. She thinks of the duets she and her sister, the musical one, the one who carried the tune, played there, with Kate playing the easy bass chords, making all the mistakes.

She rises and goes over to the leather sofa where her sister and she retreated, lying side by side, reading the same book, dreaming the same adolescent dreams.

Everything they had was the same: the Clark's shoes with the crepe soles, the smocked dresses with the pants to match, the Didee dolls. Sometimes her sister would protest, wanting to wear something different from her, but Kate did not let her. They slept in the same room, side-by-side, read the same books, discovered Dostoyevsky together, and copied out, in their hard-backed black notebooks, the same long passages of Ivan's speeches about the existence of Evil.

Automatically, she falls upon what her mother calls the Chesterfield, though she is not sure that is the proper name for a sofa of this kind. She smells the smoke-filled leather, her father's smell.

Instinctively, she runs her hand down between the cushions and the back of the sofa—fishing, they called it—and pulls out more or less the same things that would have been there years ago: a Bic, a coin, a piece of cellophane rolled into a ball, and a knife.

Listening to the muffled, lonely sounds of the isolated house, a distant shout in the street, the jangle of a bell on a bicycle, she realizes what is missing: the voice of her sister calling out, "Follow me, follow me."

II

"CAN I GET YOU ANYTHING, Dr. Marais?" the young nurse asks. She sits at his bedside. She knits. A diligent nurse, Louis thinks, too diligent. She watches him with tears in her violet eyes. He has no use for sympathy. What is she doing in the bloody intensive care unit? She looks too young to him. Not that he is complaining: the younger, the less experienced, the better.

But the young nurse gets on his nerves. She hovers over his bed. Louis prefers the older, fatter, Afrikaans one. She comes at night and falls asleep in the armchair against the wall. He smells the sweat. The older one is easier to handle. She eats half a packet of Cadbury's chocolate biscuits in the blue light. He hears the rustling, the crunching, and then the stertorous breathing.

He has even been able to climb out of his bed. He has walked to the window to stretch his legs. He has done a few quick knee-bends, to tone up the muscles, for when he will be able to move out of here. For when he will be able to move out into the night.

The older nurse doesn't bother him with unnecessary questions. The others ask him questions which are beside the point. They lead nowhere. They extrapolate. He is what he is. They invent connections. That is their business: connections. He understands signs, symptoms, and diagnoses. Most people are guilty of bad conduct. He doesn't ask himself about the nature of evil. He doesn't ask himself about anything. Mostly his mind is a blank tape. All he knows is that he has been disappointed in love. Nothing else applies.

Certain things have happened. More than he intends to mention. He will keep certain facts to himself. He knows what must have occurred. He has overheard snatches of conversation, fragments of the nurses' patter. He has put the pieces together. Certain scenes are clear in his mind. He keeps that to himself too, because of *die kinders*. He wants to go back to them. It's the one thing he wants. But he has decided the best place for him, at the moment, considering the circumstances, is right here, in this hospital bed. Here he is quiet and safe and still.

He wonders how long he has been lying in this room with the green paint and sheets. He has lost count: there are missing moments, gaps in his recollections, silences. Time has slowed. Long days, even longer nights. Greater boredom, even, than he has ever endured. He has so often been bored. The world has become increasingly abstract. His own body has become abstract. He thinks about where his body ends and the air begins.

Oh, he eats, he urinates, he defecates. He lets the nurses wash him. They turn him, rub him down with alcohol, bring his food. They swab his ears. Never has he had someone handle his body so carefully. His body hardly belongs to him. He sees it at a distance in the hands of these bleached attendants. Once in a while he slips his hand down and feels his sex stiffen, but his sex could almost be someone else's: an animal with a life of its own. A fox. He wakes at night in the silence of the hospital. He feels himself spin like a top. He leaves this body, this empty husk, abandoned.

It is not entirely unpleasant. Never has he been able to rest like this. Never has he had time to lie and think back on his life. Never has he been able to lie so still for days. He wonders how much longer they will allow him to lie here. What will happen next?

He remembers extraneous details: the mini-tractor in the shed, the smell of grease, night benches in the park, his hands beneath his thighs, Mr. Potgieter's hands on the piano keys, certain words: "What are you doing to me?" He remembers how Mr. Potgieter would smoke a cigarette. He held it between thumb and finger like a pencil. He sucked like a kid taking a first puff, like a kiss. Voluptuously.

Sometimes, lying here in his hospital bed, Louis hears his mother's voice calling him: "*Boetie*, you hear me! I know you can hear me! Oh, you know me, you do *Boetie*, don't pretend you're not awake! You don't fool me! I've got a whole lot to tell you, and I won't let you go deaf on me!" She always spoke with exclamation points at the end of her sentences. She kept him at the table after dinner, to tell him what he did not want to know. She confided in him, him alone. She said he was the only one who understood. She talked endlessly, and she smoked. He would make her go outside to smoke. "Don't smoke, Ma, it's not good for you." He knew that even then. He keeps gray lungs in formaldehyde on the mantelpiece to remind *die kinders* never to smoke.

He knows he has to be careful if he wants to see them again. If he wants to go back to his house. He hardly ever moves. If he can keep still long enough, he believes they will stop the questions.

One image especially comes back. He sees the hall at Crossways, the mirror, the low *kist*, with the brass fittings, the grandfather clock and the china cabinet against the wall, with the shell-shaped cups. He sees the gleam of the curving bannister, the black telephone in the stairwell. A radiance fills the hall. But he knows that is impossible. That hall is dark, gloomy.

Past events have become more real. People come and go at his bedside, dark, whispering shadows. Sometimes he sees monstrous forms, misshapen figures. They lean over him. They crouch on his chest: animals, devils, ghosts. He has had this impression before. He remembers seeing lions on the top of his cupboard as a boy. Lions? Also an owl. Many owls. He would dream of owls in the rafters. He listens for footsteps in the corridor, for whoever might be coming.

Sometimes, he longs to rise and move about. He thinks of the silver Mercedes, his mother-in-law's wedding present. He misses his car. He misses the strength of it, the surge of the engine. Could it be repaired? The damage was only on one side. He has the spare keys in a pocket, somewhere. He would like to drive his car again. He always liked to drive.

He remembers padding around the big bedroom with the velvet pelmets. He remembers stumbling around in the half-dark, careful not to wake Marion. He would go downstairs barefooted. It was the moment he liked best in that house. The day's heat would be coming. He wandered through the dark house, alone, in silence. The familiar things took on a new shape. They seemed released of their weight. He would sit on the striped swing seat on the veranda. John would bring him a cup of milky coffee, a hard-boiled egg, salt in a saucer. The trees grew out of darkness. His thoughts became ordered, clear. A bird sang through them: "Keep it! keep it!"

He remembers getting into the contained space of his car. He drove alone with the top down. The radio blared. The dawn wind blew on his face. It lifted his heart. *Lekker, man.* He drove to the hospital along the wide road in gold light. He swung into the fast lane. He drove with the gold light in his face, the music blaring, a hard-boiled egg in his hand. He would crack it on the steering wheel, swallow it down.

Now he smells the odor of earth. He smells the leaves on the trees. He smells the dust, which rises in great gusts with the spring wind. The air might fill the emptiness within him, the aching boredom. But he lies still, still. He doesn't answer their questions. They speak of ambivalence to life. They look for reasons which are beside the point. No one offers comfort. They never have.

Stille water, deeper grond, onder draai die duivel rond, his mother would say. She stared at his face. He inherited his face from his father. He looks alright, always has, he knows. His father had many plans. If certain deals had worked out, his father said. He remembers following him barefoot, down the dark corridor. He sees himself looking over his shoulder, nappie sagging. A first memory or perhaps an old photograph. His mother wanted to know what he was thinking, doing. "What are you doing, Louis?" she called through the closed door of the *uithuis.* He remembers the smell of shit and lime, the deep black double *gat.*

He learned to keep his thoughts to himself. He was a secretive child. He knew how to use a smile to disarm. His mother's yearnings suffused his childhood. When he looked at the world around him he thought an error had been made. It was an error he intended to rectify any way he could. He would have no mercy on whatever it was that had robbed him of his due. He would show the fat *rooineks* what he could do!

He knows the separate world of the hospital well, after all, the smells, the routine, the lingo. Dr. Walsh came with the ink blots, the questions. "Have you ever tried to, uhm, harm yourself?" he wanted to know.

Louis said, "You talking about suicidal ideation?" He had to laugh at his face. Intelligence problem, there. A psychiatrist, hardly a doctor, a muddled man of the mind.

All he could see in his bloody ink blots were cocks. He wasn't going to tell him that, obviously. He hears the comings and goings of the nurses, their voices, laughter. He listens for footsteps, visitors. Not many visitors. Serge has not been near him. His siblings have not lingered. No surprise there. Nor does it displease him. He hardly remembers their names: Francois, Eugene, Carl, Sarie, Maritijie. Each added child was a slap in the face, an insult: more work, more noise, more expense. He doesn't remember loving his mother, only wanting to escape the burden of her love.

Louis wonders about Marion's mother. What is she planning to do? He sees her in her silk jersey skirt, the powdered face, the mauve lipstick, the fine arch of the eyebrows. He can still smell her perfume. And he thinks of the younger sister, Kate. Will she have come out here? He hasn't seen her for a while. The same dark hair except longer, the same high-headed walk, the same voice. Almost identical, the younger sister, though not as soft and supple as the older one. Never was.

He has been disappointed in love.

He had thought of her as perfect, his Marion. "Miss Marion" he had called her sometimes, or even "Maid Marion, My Maid Marion, Mistress Marion, Madame Marion" or sometimes in anger, "Marion, the martyr." The truth is, he would have liked to bow down to her. Secretly, in his heart, he had thought of her as holy.

He thinks of his children: Mark, his eldest, his boy, with his big solemn eyes, fat cheeks; his little Lydia, with her pigtails and her skinny legs; and his baby, Deidre, his favorite one, his beauty. He thinks of her fine, white-gold hair. He thinks of her light, light eyes, his eyes. She's the one who looks the most like him, a tiny version of her father, with something of his stance already, his expressions—everyone commented on it. Chip off the old block, Marion would say, when the baby screamed. He sees the children move through the garden as if in slow motion, coming toward him, arms outstretched. He would like to hold them in his arms. He remembers carrying his baby on his shoulders. He remembers running through the grass, barefoot. He says her name aloud. He remembers the sound of her voice calling his name. He looks out the window. The gray sky is lit up for a moment before the night. A time of hope, it was, before everything went wrong.

III

On Marion's last afternoon, John carried the tea tray as usual into the lounge, when the many clocks chimed four, shuffling in his sand-shoes, holes on the sides, which give a little air to his cramped toes. He relies on memory to guide him across the parquet floor, around the furniture which he knows intimately, having kept it polished for so long. He doesn't trust the many other servants, *skelms*, common rubbish, to do anything properly, anymore.

The Wise Ones of his tribe used to say that the human race was so troublesome because people were born upside down. Perhaps, if man were born with his feet more firmly planted on the ground his head would be less full of rubbish—foolish notions and desires that bring sadness and death.

All they want is to use the machines the white man has brought them, and nothing good can come from such machines, in the end, he is certain, nothing but waste and destruction. He has always refused to use the machines, not the one that grinds up the oranges and spits out a thin trickle of juice, nor the one that sucks up the dust with a dreadful roar, nor the one that hides the plates in the dark where they cannot be found. The machines the white man has brought them, the guns he has sold them, have caused nothing but harm.

He always insists on taking in the tray himself, though his sight is not as good as it used to be. He shuffles into the usually silent room with only the sound of his starched, rustling uniform, the chink of the cups, the shrilling of the cicadas, and the water gurgling over the wall. He checks, feeling with his hands to make sure the teapot in its knitted tea-cozy, the requisite number of cups, the forks and teaspoons, the hot buttered scones, the jam pot, and the starched linen napkins are all there.

It was as he put down the tray on the coffee table he had polished that morning to a high shine, that he became aware of the weeping sound. He stood there, listening. Miss Marion was sitting on the yellow silk settee with her cocker spaniel, Rosie, at her feet. She was holding a letter and weeping.

He stood there for a moment, clucked his tongue, and shook his head. The curtains were open, and there was sunlight in the room. He could hear a dove cooing and one of the servants singing about a lion, of all things. As if that one knew anything about lions! He would probably poison himself with the wrong berry if you left him in the bush for more than five minutes. That one has probably never seen a lion and has done nothing for years but lounge about under the trees, fall asleep in the shade, and most probably, smoke his *dagga*.

"What is it?" he asked Miss Marion, but she did not reply, and though he stood there for a long while, waiting and peering through the gloom of his blinded eyes, she did not tell him, as she usually did, what was in her heart.

When John's beloved first wife and their two children—the youngest one still so small she had her uncut "hair of innocence"—were poisoned by an envious neighbor, he decided that the reason for him to go on living was to look after Julia Kempden and her two little girls, Marion and Kate. For Julia Kempden, too, had lost her mate and was left a widow alone in this big house. John felt it his duty, now that her husband, the old *baas*, Hans Kempden, was dead, to protect this woman, his *Nkosi*, and her children, his *izinkosazana*, and he has done his best over the years to accomplish this aim.

He thought of Julia Kempden, who was now suddenly a widow, on her own and defenseless. He knows she has been snubbed by society in this city, and that her own relatives have preyed upon her over the years. John knows that they have taken advantage of his *Nkosi's* position as the wife of a successful timber merchant.

Nights he would imagine her lying alone in her large, lonely bed, as he lay in his lonely cot, and in his heart he understood her trouble, facing the innumerable days and nights. He did not blame her for turning to the bottle for solace in her sorrow, for he knows that despite her wealth, it is the small, secret sorrows of the heart that are the hardest to bear.

She has been good to him in times of sickness and in trouble, he believes, and she has been generous. She has always remembered to pay his wages on time, and she has given him a large box every Christmas, and she has gone to the pass office with him, dressed up in her pearls, to talk to the police, to make sure his pass was extended.

She shakes her head with consternation at the indignities this government inflicts upon his people, the absurdities of the pass laws, and he knows that she thinks the guttural tongue of the Afrikaans people, which the black children are now obliged to learn in the schools, is a bastard one and fit only, she says, for barbarians. He knows she prefers him to all the other servants, and that she would trust him with her life, as, indeed, he has trusted her with his. He knows that he is her Head Man, and she is his *Nkosi*. As for Miss Marion, he has always taken care of her.

But their two lives, which had been so inextricably linked by the rhythms of the old house, were slowly moving along their separate ways, for his *inkosazana* was preparing to leave this place, where he has been longer and which he knows better than anyone else.

He knows everything about Miss Marion, more than a mother knows about her child, more than a husband about his wife, more than she knows about herself. He has wiped her vomit from the floor and washed her blood from the sheets, even though that is against the rules of his tribe. He has picked up her little budgerigar and felt its fluttering wings, after she accidentally stepped on it and broke its back and crushed it. "Better like this," he had said wringing its neck.

He has saved her life several times: caught the heavy armoire in the bedroom, when it almost fell and crushed her small body; leant down and pulled her from the reeds of the fishpond, where she had fallen one summer afternoon; brought her through the scarlet fever, when she was shut up in the nursery away from everyone else for fear of contagion.

They were bound together by an intimacy which was closer than any physical bond. They listened to the same clocks ticking, the same cicadas shrilling in the silences of the long afternoons in the old house, the same water gurgling over the wall into the pool.

That afternoon, Miss Marion only told him to take the scones away and have someone eat them in the kitchen.

Later that evening, when the young *baas* had come in, John overheard bits and pieces of their conversation on the veranda, as he came and went with the drink tray.

In an unusually loud and insistent voice Miss Marion was saying, "But then you must just go and see them, and tell them it was a mistake! You must explain what really happened."

Baas Louis said, raising his voice, too, "They won't want to see me. They won't believe me. You don't understand. It's a waste of time."

"What else can you do? You must go. It's important. Just tell them there has been a terrible mistake," she said, her voice trembling.

The voices grew louder, but John could not hear anymore, as he was busy in the kitchen, supervising dinner, making sure the other servants kept the soup sufficiently hot, the plates warm, the fish not overcooked, which otherwise they were quite likely to forget. Besides, he has never been a listener at keyholes; such a thing is beneath his dignity. Nor has it been necessary. He leaves that to the aunt, whom they call Dottie. Nor is his English very good. He could not see the couple on the veranda, the defeated expression on Louis's face, or the flush of outrage in Marion's cheeks.

Later, he watched them leave for the party, a blur of black tuxedo and white dress. He saw them drift across the lawn, as they went toward the garages. Through his blinded eyes, he thought they already looked as if they were floating like ghosts.

It was after midnight when the two Afrikaans policemen knocked loudly, and John stumbled up the steps and opened the Dutch door of the house.

IV

K ATE KNEELS BESIDE HER MOTHER on the blue kneeler in the stone Anglican church. Late afternoon sunlight slants in from the high, stained-glass windows. The packed church is hot and redolent with the cloying odor of arum lilies and incense. In her black suit and feathered hat, Kate feels sweat trickle down her forehead. Her face is burning. Her mother says nothing throughout the ceremony, sitting bolt upright in her pew in her boned corset and cream ribbon-knit suit and diamonds, staring with a glassy, fixed stare, as though she, too, has turned to stone.

They stand with a rustle to sing Marion's favorite hymns, which are also Kate's, "All Things Bright and Beautiful," and "Jerusalem." "In the beauty of the lilies, Christ was born, across the sea," Kate tries to sing, the words choking her like water.

Kate listens to the stout minister who stands before the altar eulogizing in his white robes. She remembers him from the chapel at school. He speaks of Marion's love of languages, music, children, and those in distress. He tells a story about the wounded animals she collected: the puppy half-drowned in a ditch, the stray cats, the wounded birds, the monkey who followed her around the lawn until he turned vicious and bit her.

Kate is reminded of the other strays Marion took into their home: the young girl who was not being treated kindly by the family where she worked, who had slept in the spare room for months on end and had to be told to take a bath; the hitchhiker she had brought home for Sunday dinner, who had eaten half the roast; the woman who thought she was Josephine and had to be called "Empress," whom she brought in for tea and cake and who lingered through the evening for drinks.

Her sister was not religious but thought of her religion as absorbing and carrying around the pain of others. She even had a name for it, which had appeared to her in a dream. She said it was called "Epone."

The minister speaks of her calm beauty and its beneficent influence. Marion, Kate thinks, probably didn't see herself in that way; vagueness, indecisiveness was more likely. But Kate remembers the high, delicate head, the small, pale, uncertain mouth, the small chin, and the blue lids. With her luminous, wide-spaced eyes, her lush eyelashes, her lips slightly open, her soft dark curls, she looked to Kate like one of Pontormo's late Mannerist angels.

Marion had studied art and languages at Witwatersrand University in Johannesburg, while Kate was still at boarding school. She came home every evening to crotchet with her mother and her aunt, sitting in the wicker furniture, which the architect had had sent from California for the veranda. She drove her mother and aunt to chapel at Kate's school on Sundays and then took them all out for lunch at the Oasis.

After Marion graduated, she found a job working in a gallery in Johannesburg, where her tact with difficult clients,

Kate is certain, her quiet unobtrusive presence, and her sweet low voice on the telephone must have taken her far.

Kate remembers how her mother told her two girls after their father had died, when Kate was seven and Marion nine years old, "Now you are all I have left in the world."

Kate stands in the garden at Crossways, vaguely aware of wet jacarandas, goldenrod, the damp, dark earth. Above the blue hills, the sky is streaked with red. It has rained in the night, a sudden spring storm. She breathes in the smell of damp earth.

Kate has seen the wedding photographs of her parents standing on this lawn at Crossways, her father, twenty years older than her mother, looking pleased with himself in a double-breasted suit, his arm slung carelessly around her mother's shoulders, and her young mother in a brown suit, clasping a bunch of white roses, her dark hair parted down the middle and her lovely face lifted up to the light.

Kate thinks of the strange way this place was built. Their father had hired a deaf architect, who read lips and spoke in a high-pitched incomprehensible voice, and was much in demand at the time. Her father considered himself fortunate when the architect accepted his low offer.

He told him what he wanted as clearly and succinctly as possible: something plain and simple, easy to keep up, economical, a small, sunny English cottage with a thatched roof and roses growing up the walls.

Her father came from a German family of prudent tradespeople where thrift was considered a virtue. His mother, she was told, always wore her money bag under her voluminous skirts on the train for fear of robbers.

Her father gave instructions to the architect and thought he had understood. He left him to it. He was a busy man, after all. All his brothers were in the timber business, until one of them was killed during the war, fighting the Italians in North Africa.

Either the architect couldn't understand, or chose not to. He built a sprawling, red-brick house, south-facing and dark, with a flat roof and a high wall on one side, where the water rises from the pool and cascades back down with a sound which fills all the rooms. He probably imagined, in his silent world, that the noise would be soporific, but it kept her father awake in the night.

The architect even ordered a baby grand piano for the lounge. Her father had mentioned something about acquiring some furniture which might be appropriate and made a small allowance for this. He presumed the architect conjured up the sounds the piano would make, though he himself had never learned to play and had a tin ear.

The architect terraced the flat veld with brick walls, planted with plumbago, which cascaded down in melancholy blue waves to the jacarandas at the bottom of the garden. He laid out the rock garden with various kinds of expensive cacti. He installed a tennis court and trained morning glory to grow up the wire. In the bottom half of the garden, he landscaped a nine-hole golf course. Her father managed with difficulty to preserve most of the original jacarandas by arriving one afternoon during the construction in time to throw his arms around the trunk of one of them.

It was in these trees that John had told the sisters that the *Tokolosh* hid. They had to be careful not to displease him, or he might carry them away in their beds, which were not put up on wedges. The tricky *Tokolosh* was ready to pounce, to put a curse on them, to change them into two different girls. He came in disguises and hid in many places, but one tree in particular was his favorite. They never went near it.

Once, they saw the evil one in the night in the form of a witch. He was shining a light through the bay window into the nursery. He had put a curse on them so that they could not move an inch, or call out for help.

She knows many of the people who have returned to the house after the funeral. She sees them very clearly, the outlines of their dark clothes distinct. In the shadows of the evening light, she watches them float across the lawn and hover near the trestletable with the flowers and the French champagne and the canapes or wander, plates in hand, over to the pool in small, sad groups, heads bowed, whispering. They come up to Kate and shake her hand and murmur something awkwardly in her ear. "So very, very sorry," they say.

Among them is their aunt Dottie, the edge of her black Leghorn hat trembling as she totters across the lawn on brittle legs, her high heels digging into the damp earth, sucking a large peppermint to guard against bad breath, as she kisses Kate's cheek; their Uncle Charles, grown stout and pale, who kisses her and holds onto her hands for a moment too long, until his wife, a nurse, her bandy legs showing beneath her brown skirt, tells him to come along now.

There are many of her sister's old school friends and even their headmistress, bent now, her face a web of wrinkles. There is John, of course, well over six feet, who has grown so frail and thin over his many years of service that the bones of his narrow face seem almost visible through his shiny skin. He has sat at the back of the church, rocking back and forth, keening and wiping tears from his eyes.

There are Marion's three children, who follow John across the lawn: Mark and Lydia, six and four years old, and the baby, Deidre, only two-and-a-half. The two girls are in their identical, pale, smocked dresses, pants to match, and their patent-leather shoes, drifting after John under the jacarandas, dangling rag dolls by the arm. Mark wears blue shorts and Clark's sandals, as Marion and Kate did as girls. The dog, Rosie, zigzags beside them, nose to the ground. Already, Kate thinks, they have the blank tear-stained faces of neglected children. She watches John swing the baby girl onto his back and carry her into the flowers.

There are others Kate knows less well: her sister's husband's large family, all sweating in thick, dark clothes and hovering near the food, the innumerable white-blond brothers and sisters, their stout wives, thin husbands, and their noisy children, who have arrived from their farms in the Great Karoo together.

A reddish-haired man, who looks flustered, his pale, freckled skin, flushed, emerges suddenly from behind the big bowl of delphiniums. He is wearing a tweed jacket and khaki pants, which appear too heavy for the weather. A slight man, he seems in a hurry. He clasps her hand fervently in both his damp palms, as her uncle did, and says he is so glad to see her again. She stares into his shifting, chestnut-brown eyes, the whites slightly dirty, and tries to remember his name.

"We met in Geneva with your sister," he explains.

"Of course, of course."

Kate now remembers him, the accountant, Malachy, pulling out the heavy chair with the carved arms for her sister in that formal dining room at the hotel. What was its name? White water churned down the narrow gorge below their window.

He says, "I need to show you something, and soon. It's important." When she promises to call him, he rushes off in his jacket with the padded shoulders, much too large for him.

Then a tall, dark-haired man, who looks vaguely familiar, comes up and introduces himself.

"A friend of Louis's, Serge," he explains. "We were at medical school together."

"Of course, of course," Kate says again. She remembers him, the anaesthetist. He is the one who brought Louis to the house that first time. She sat next to him at the dinner table and asked him about Louis. What was it he had said? They had begun their medical training together, and he had caught Louis when he fainted, the first time they showed them a cadaver. He told her that Louis was not very tactful—blunt, rather, and unrestrained in his comments and actions, with no time for humbug. Serge said he tried to keep him out of trouble.

"Your sister was such a loving woman, so generous, kind, and intelligent. We shared a love of Proust, you know?" he says now.

"You did?"

He gives her his number, and she makes a show of slipping it into her purse. She promises to call but silently decides against it.

She realizes with a shock that he resembles her sister somewhat: tall, broad-shouldered, dark-haired, and luminous-eyed.

All that is over now, or is it? Kate wonders. She will wake every morning to see her sister lifting up her small face to her, obligingly, as though she, too, wished to show her that she was really dead.

V

"YOU FEELING COMFORTABLE, Dr. Marais?" the young nurse asks Louis once again.

That was his forte: keeping his patients comfortable after operating on them. He was very thorough, had to be: it was concentration that had got him through it; concentration, and a good memory. And Mr. Potgieter. He couldn't have done it without Pottie. He remembers Pottie driving all the way out to his mother's house in his battered car, risking the rutted roads to talk to his mother. A thin, tall man, he must have stooped, bowed his head, his old brown hat in his hands, as he came in the door, probably turning the hat around by the brim.

"Not disturbing, I hope?" His mother at the stove in her apron, frying eggs, eyed him suspiciously. She had a mole on her chin. Pottie told her her eldest son was definitely "university material."

"University material?" his mother had said. She wiped her hands on her apron. She cleared off the dishes. She offered him a cup of tea from the brown teapot at the kitchen table. She smoked one of his cigarettes. His father was heaven knows where.

Too bad about Pottie. He was a good man, unlike so many others. He isn't going to think about that.

Concentration was most important. He had passed his "matric" at sixteen. He had been in a hurry to finish school, once he knew there was hope of leaving home, once there was hope of going on to the university. It was concentration that had done it.

It was work, work, from the start. How much of his life has been hard work! He has been working since he could walk. He made his bed when he was four. No time off: even with the measles, his mother had him up and at it. She wanted him to do all the things his father had never done. She taught him to do all the things a man should know how to do. The wood he chopped, the drains he unplugged, the garbage he burned, the snakes he killed—puff adders, ringhals, shutting his eyes, terrified, and beating with a stick, the enamel basin with the chipped lip he held when she was sick. He would turn away so as not be sick himself. Other things, too: stumbling about barefoot, shivering with fever in his thin jersey, the gray sleeve unravelling, his teeth chattering. "Ma, I'm sick!" he would croak in the early morning in the half-dark, the smells of burning porridge.

She was a terrible cook. She smoked while she cooked, the ash tray at her side, ashes falling in the eggs. She served something ghastly she called sweet and sour beans, which made him want to puke. She put sugar into everything, the beetroot salad, the spaghetti, even the steak, on the rare occasions she served steak. She sprinkled sugar on the lamb chops when they slaughtered a sheep for a special occasion. She made *koeksisters*, dripping in oil and coated with sugar that glistened like flies' wings. She made him sit at the table and finish the food on his plate in that breathless, shotgun house in the middle of nowhere.

The first home he remembers was the farm where his father worked for fifty pounds a year. It belonged to a Jewish man. It was near a *dorp* in the Great Karoo. The land all around was flattened by blinding light. In the hot afternoons mirages danced in the distance. The house had a corrugated iron roof. It was boiling in summer and freezing in winter, the wind blowing all year round. Nothing there but heat, smoke, and the fine, red dust, carried by the wind across barren spaces. Nothing there but silence, so deep it was a constant hum in his ears.

The yard backed onto yellow veld. The wind blew the dust against the windows. It was in his hair, his ears, his mouth. Sometimes he dreamed of being buried in dust like a frog. Dust lay on the surfaces of the house like a shroud. The house was filled with dust and his mother's cigarette smoke. He built some rabbit cages out back. He would go out there and talk to the rabbits, small, wet, blind things curled up like grubs, rabbits no one wanted. He fed them, but they didn't live.

That's how he started with the school work. Going to school was his way out. Going to school was his salvation, even if it meant walking for miles, on cracked soil, thorns in the soles of his feet. He trudged over hot, hard ground in the summer without a hat or shoes. He set out for school in the dark, cold winter mornings in his cotton shirt and short pants without a blazer. More often than not, his head was shaved because of the ringworm. The sound of his pants, swishing against his legs as he strode off, was his only company. His nose ran. He was always the first to arrive. On entering, he would blow on his hands, stamp his bare feet, and shiver.

He would do anything for the teachers to stay on late at school in the afternoons. "Give me some lines to memorize, please," he would beg. Pottie would stare at him with wonderment. "Lines! No one has ever asked me for lines!"

he would say and shake his head. Louis learned all of the "Ancient Mariner" not even in his native Afrikaans, by heart: "Water, water everywhere, nor any drop to drink." He had never seen either the sea, or an albatross.

Now Louis remembers Pottie's wild red hair. He remembers his pale blue eyes, the tender freckled skin, the white-tipped eyelashes, the long white fingers, the not-so-clean nails. Other things, too.

Memorizing lines was wonderfully easy for him. He was blessed with a photographic memory. He could see the pages before him. He could read them. The other boys stared at him, open-mouthed. They thought it was magic. They didn't understand how to sit at your own wooden desk and listen to a teacher could be paradise. Even with the engravings of a hundred boys' names in the desklid, with gum stuck underneath and sometimes worse things, but away from the noise of *die kinders*, the stench of dirty *nappies*, and out of range of the *sjambok*, was paradise. What he liked best was just to sit and stare back at the boys, at their tan legs, the blond hair, the beautiful Afrikaans boys who looked like him. He liked to listen to them talk. Their foul language made him laugh. His mother would have washed his mouth out for saying what they did: *fok* and *piel* and the wonderful one, *poep-hol*. He understood from the start that the dark, heavy guttural *gat* words were about sex and desire.

He had never been caned at school. He was the only boy in the class who avoided it. He knew how to be careful. He knew the right things to say. He didn't understand why the other boys chanted at the end of the term, "No more sitting on the hard old bench." Sitting there was safe, if you were careful. All you had to do was give the right answers and say, "*Ja, Meneer.*"

He hated holidays, his mother's screams and the insults. Even homework, *man*, was heaven. It was one thing his mother let him do. She would clear off one end of the thick wooden table for him. He sat there, at the clean end, out of the smoke. He bit on the end of a pencil, staring at sums and making them come out right. It was better than grating cheese or chopping onions, than lifting firewood for the stove, changing *nappies*, or, for no reason he could ascertain, getting a bloody hiding with the *sjambok*. Even worse were the sudden, fierce hugs, the hot breath on the neck, the words of endearment. *Liefste Boetie, ons bring rosies, rosies blink met more dou*, she would croon in his ear, as if there were roses around there. She would turn the old *tannie* song into his own.

He remembers the afternoon his mother told him she would teach him something new, something he would need to know to be a man. She called it practicing. "*Kom Boetie,*" she said and stubbed out her cigarette. She took him out the back of the house into the deep shadows of the porch, where the rabbit cages used to be. He can still taste the flick of her tongue in his mouth, oily as a smoked fish. He can smell her odor of talcum powder and sweat. He can still feel himself sinking, sinking into her abundant flesh, the heavy breasts, the full stomach, the thrust of the pubic bone hard as a stone against him. It was the unexpectedness, the arbitrariness of it all, that were unbearable: the never knowing or being able to control what was coming next, the caress or the blow on the head.

VI

KATE'S MOTHER, JULIA, LAYS DOWN HER KNITTING NEEDLES. She and her sister Dottie are both knitting cardigans for Marion's children on this late spring afternoon. Her mother says they will have to make the visit to the clinic at some point. Might as well get it over with. Not far to go, after all, just down the road.

A breeze shifts the light things in the room, the fronds of the maidenhair fern in the pot where Kate long ago dared Marion to pee, the petals of the dusty proteas in the old brass pot on the mantelpiece, the leaves of her mother's paperback, which lies on the desk between the French windows. She is still reading Barbara Cartland!

"You will come with us, of course?" her mother asks Kate, who sits beside her and her aunt on the silk-covered sofa.

She cannot think of what to say. She has a sore on the side of her mouth, and she touches it with the tip of her tongue. She looks at the sunlight, which floods the floor, and wonders if the wood were not once lighter than this. She remembers it as honey-colored beneath their patent-leather shoes. She looks around the vast, sunlit room and thinks of her three small, shady rooms in Paris. She stares at her mother's powdered face. Though now ravaged, she is still, at sixty, a beautiful woman. She holds her head high with unmistakable authority. Her mother is not a woman whose desires one ignores easily.

"If you want me to," Kate says and folds her hands in her lap.

"And you might put on something a little less lugubrious, darling," she says looking at Kate's clothes.

She is still wearing the black linen skirt and long-sleeved crepe de chine blouse she bought in Paris for her sister's funeral, though it is more than a week since the funeral. She rarely spends money on clothes and passes much of her life in blue jeans and *takkies*, but for some reason she had bought a black linen suit and even a black feathered hat with greenish glints, as though the elegant, expensive clothes could protect her.

Her mother looks hard at her and adds, "And put on a little lipstick, will you? You look a bit anemic."

Kate wants to remind her that she is now thirty-six years old, that she has been living on her own in Paris since she was twenty, and that she has translated several difficult French books into English, but instead she swallows and says nothing. She touches the pins which hold her dark, shoulder-length hair into place at the back of her head, and then with a sigh takes out her pale lipstick from her loose-weave basket and without looking in a mirror quickly smears a touch of color on her lips.

Dottie says, "I'm sure Marion would want us to go, Jule." Dottie calls her younger sister Jule, because she was a tomboy in her youth. Dottie has cut her gray-white hair short and wears it in tight, permed curls about her flushed face. At sixty-three she suffers from high blood pressure, and her hands tremble as she moves them through the air.

Kate sees her sister's face in the early spring light glimmering with tears. She remembers sitting at her side on the edge of the Bernini fountain in Rome at the bottom of the Spanish Steps, the swallows circling above in a calm blue sky, the sound of water flowing. She would do anything to have that moment back, to hold her sister again in her arms, to keep her safe. It is her sister's physical presence she misses now in this vast, empty room.

Their mother would laugh at Kate as she followed her sister around as a child. She would taunt, "I had a little shadow, goes in and out with me, and what can be the use of it, is hard for me to see."

Now she follows her mother, as she rises stiffly from the silk-covered sofa. Her mother still stands erect and slim in her triple-string pearl necklace and drop-pearl earrings, the nose straight, the lips thin. She tells Dottie to have John watch the children while they are at the clinic.

"Tell him to take them into the kitchen with him. I don't want them outside near the pool," she says. She turns to Kate and lowers her voice, "The children adore him, of course, as you two did, but I'm always afraid one of them might fall in. He's a bit of a problem. Too old really to do anything at all. Puts sugar instead of salt in the soup. Blunders around the kitchen, driving all the other servants crazy, bossing them around. None of them will stay. None of the maids can stand him. But what can we do?"

"But we couldn't do without him, could we?" Kate asks.

Her mother sighs. "Can't pension him off. Doesn't want to go back to his homeland. You remember the daughter who teaches? Done well for herself. Teaches at Fort Hare now. Snubs him because he can't write or read and doesn't have a clue how old he is."

"How old do you think?" Kate asks.

"Eighty, perhaps? Might even be ninety. Who knows? Anyway a real nineteenth-century man and stubborn as a mule."

Dottie goes to give the instructions and to fetch her sister's shawl, though the afternoon is warm, the light dazzling. When she comes back into the sunken lounge, she stands waiting for them in the doorway, a dark, slim form in her silk jersey skirt and shirt with the light behind her. She has always been thin and maintains she weighed a hundred pounds when she turned twenty-one, though she is tall. Like Kate she has never married. She has lived with her younger sister since Kate's father's death.

Kate has been at her mother's home for more than a week now. Her mother stands beside her, chin lifted, the dark curls soft and thick, the hazel eyes large and bright.

"Have you told Wilson to bring up the car?" Julia asks Dottie in her loud voice.

Wilson, a light-skinned Xhosa in his early forties, drives them in the black Jaguar down the long driveway under the alley of jacarandas and through the white gate. Kate sits in the back between her mother and her aunt in a cloud of their perfume, listening to the tinkle of their bracelets—her aunt wears copper to ward off rheumatism—the soft sighs of their silk jersey dresses, their gossip about the various people in their lives. She remembers as a child finding this gossip so fascinating that she would ask them to stop talking, if she had to leave the veranda and go to the bathroom.

Now they are talking about Louis. "The mother was impossible, of course—let herself go completely. Do you remember the hat she wore to the wedding? My dear!"

Kate remembers Wilson telling her and Marion that if things were to go on as they were in this country, he would simply have to fold his arms one day. She remembers him saying, "We thought we could talk to the white man and he would listen, but we were wrong."

VII

THE NURSE TELLS HIM his mother-in-law will be visiting this afternoon. She is coming with her sister and her remaining child, his sister-in-law.

He says nothing to that, closes his eyes. What are they coming for? What do they want with him now?

He remembers the first time he saw the mother at the public pool, when she came to fetch the girls. Someone had told him she drank. All her diamonds flashed, and the big pearls, which hung from her earlobes, glistened. He thought she looked like an alkie, but beautiful. He knew the signs. She had that glitter in the eye, the veins too visible, the legs too slender.

Once, he saw Marion almost hit her head at the public pool. Afterwards he wondered why she and her sister went there. They had one of their own, after all. It may have been the boys. There were often boys clustering around them. He didn't like that. He observed the hours when they came, and went whenever he thought they might be there, the early hours of the afternoon, when the swimming heats were held. He would abandon his books or even skip a lecture to go down to the big pool. It wasn't far from where he was doing his medical training. There were factories around there. Vendors sold things on the street. Not a fancy area. It wasn't far, either, from where his friend Serge had found a flat. He would sit on the benches and watch.

He had never done anything like that before. Oh, he had been out with a few girls. One with the name of a flower had been keen on him. He couldn't remember much about her, Strillie, perhaps, short for Strelitzia, something odd like that. He hadn't had much time for girls. He knew what to say. He saw their quick little glances of appraisal when they looked him over. He didn't mind that.

He would write it down in his diary if he had the good luck to spot them. M.K. and K.K. he wrote, when he had found out their names. He wrote down if they won the competitions.

Both girls were divers. M.K. did the swallow, but her best dive, the one which gave him the thrill, was the back flip. She would walk out to the end of the board and turn quickly, gripping the edge with her long toes. She concentrated. She stood there arms raised, beautifully balanced. She sprang up into the air. She strained skywards with her fingertips, rising high from the matted board. She hung in the air a moment, as if she had discovered the gift of flight. She twisted. Then she plummeted, down, down, dangerously close to the end of the board, going through blue air and blue water. She was gone, as though forever. He waited, holding his breath. Then there would be the splash and the delighted surprise of the dark head surfacing, hair streaming.

Once, she had miscalculated, staying too close to the end of the board, a hairbreadth away. There was dead quiet in the crowd. He could hardly breathe. He wrote it down in his diary. Diligently, he wrote down his progress with his studies, his grades. He kept a record of the exercise he took, of what he ate. He always kept himself fit, a flat stomach, a muscled back, strong arms.

Of course, he didn't dare approach them. You would have had to be rich and famous to approach girls like that. There was no possibility for him. Not with his accent, not speaking the way he spoke, not coming where he came from. He put them up on a pedestal, one that he later realized was dangerously high.

He had no money at all, no lineage, though his mother was a du Toit from an old French Huguenot family. She even had a small dowry. But she had married his father for love, she said, a handsome man, with blond sideburns, a lovely mustache, and the easy ways of a traveling salesman.

Louis has seen small, shadowy wedding photos, the edges curling. His mother looks slim and shy. Her head is covered with a veil. Her satin dress falls in a pool around her feet. She stares up at his father. Admiration lights up her small, gray eyes.

His father lost his job on the South African railways because of some scandal that involved a black man. That was all he could ever find out. His parents were obliged to go back to his mother's family farm in the Cape Province. Louis was born there, a love child, named after French kings, less than nine months after the wedding.

His father knew little about farming, or any other useful occupation, but he always had big plans. He was a talker, a dreamer, and when the dreams didn't pan out, a drinker. Louis followed him around when he was home. His father would send him off to the back door of the local hotel to fetch a couple of bottles. It was their secret. His mother's family eventually sent them off to manage on their own.

He remembers his young mother in her apron. She rushes down the corridor to greet his father with flushed cheeks, flour on the tips of her fingers. His father staggers into the hall, late at night. His mother is in tears. "Why you crying, Ma?"

She was up before dawn. She did the accounts at night, ashtray at hand. She had a head for figures. She raised the chickens, pigs. She grew vegetables, mostly gem squash, pumpkins, for the sugared pumpkin fritters he had to eat, and dusty corn. She was the one who knew about the sheep, which ones to slaughter, which ones had the best ribs. She even knew how to repair the farm tools and the wind pump. She hired and fired the farm hands. She squeezed the work out of them by screaming at them while his father became increasingly drunk and wandered off.

When he came back from school, she sent him to find his father. "And get me a pack of cigarettes," she snapped and took a sip of water from the canvas water bottle she kept tied around her waist. He dragged his small bare feet down the dirt road, slinking along in silence, shamefaced. He stayed in the shadows under the straggly oak trees, as though he were the one at fault. He would find his father sitting in the shade of the bougainvillea on the veranda at the hotel. He would be drinking Castle beer, one after the other. More than likely, some young woman, or sometimes one not so young, sat on his knees.

His mother grew fat. She wore an old battered straw hat which she tied under her chin. Her skin turned yellow and wrinkled with sun and smoke and rage. She stood in the *mielies*, in her loose black dress, waving her flabby arms about furiously. She ran the farm and the household on nothing. After droughts, when the veld turned to desert, she had fences put up and then more fences, shifting sheep back and forth.

She scraped and skimped. She knitted school jerseys for him at night, ran up curtains, put up *konfyt*, lay on the bed and screamed for the pan. She vomited green bile. She made babies, one after the other: puny, puking things. There were six of them left. The deaths were a relief to her. "Why do you keep doing it, Ma?" he asked. "God's will," she said, but he knew it wasn't that. He heard things at night through the thin walls. He didn't think God had anything to do with that. Babies crawled around the house like vermin, burrowing, sucking, and shitting.

Sundays, his mother played the organ in the Dutch Reformed Church, in a clean, ironed dress, hair punished with pins. He sat beside her, pumped the organ. In her loneliness and loss she turned to him, her eldest, cleverest son.

But even as a medical student, he considered these two girls at the pool out of reach. Tall, slender, dark-haired girls with the olive skin that did not burn or peel in the sun as his did. Between heats they lay languidly on the blue-green tiles, or on their towels on the grass. They barely seemed to move, and when they did, they tripped lightly over the tiles. They held their dark, sparkling heads high and still, as though balancing something precious. They hardly swung their arms or hips. They spoke softly, hardly moving their lips. When they whispered he tried to overhear what they were saying, but he could not. They seemed hardly to breathe.

He imagined the classes they must have taken in their private school: deportment(did they carry books on the top of their heads?) and elocution (did they recite poetry, perhaps in different parts, sopranos and altos?). He envisioned music classes, horseback riding, and ballet. Surely, it was not possible to walk and talk like that naturally. And they looked so clean to him, so quiet, so still. They tilted their heads upwards, eyes dreamy or shut. Or they lay on their stomachs on their big blue towels, head to head.

No one had taught him to swim as a boy, not even in the stone-walled dam, ten feet square, filled by the wind pump, where the farm boys splashed about in the brown water. He had learned when he was thirteen, the hard way. One of the bigger boys had thrown him into the dam and told him to move. Shards of light flashed in his eyes. He flung his arms about wildly, gasping and choking. He dared not open his mouth to cry for help. He swam to keep from drowning.

He has never learned to swim well, to manage the breathing, or like the sisters to slip silently through the water, fingers together. They took small sips of air from the sides of their mouths. Their clean white feet beat regularly. They swam quietly without much splash, cutting through the water like two mermaids. He watched water run off their slender bodies in silver strands as they pulled themselves up and out of the pool. They raced side by side or in relay, passing the baton. They were always entwined, arms around one another's waists or necks or sometimes, as they swam, with a leg and an arm linked for a joke. They giggled. They sputtered, going under and coming up again in their tight embrace.

At first, he could hardly tell them apart in their dark, thin racing suits, which clung to their slender, dusky bodies, their dreamy eyes brown or green, depending on the light. Their hair was glossy as a blackbird, though the younger one wore hers longer and thickly plaited.

Spotting their dark heads in the crowd of swimmers thrilled him, as though he had spotted something rare and wonderful. It was their doubleness that he found so fascinating. He would not have watched one of them alone.

Together they were a force that struck him like a blow. Now he was like everyone else, like other men. With them he grew sure he could avoid a life of shame and secrets and humiliation.

Other boys watched them from afar. Some brave ones hung around. One told him laughingly that the sisters had said they wouldn't marry anyone who hadn't read Dostoyevsky.

All he knew was medicine. He knew the physiology of the body, how the blood pumped through the veins and heart and lungs. Gradually he learned how these could weaken and fail, and what it took to fix them, if one were skilled enough. These things he learned with passion.

Then there was the bit about the older one in the local paper. She had come back from England, where she had been presented to the Queen. She had worn a pale mauve dress and a pillbox hat. That gave her an added glow, though he could hardly imagine such a thing. What was a pillbox hat? Not that he had any truck with English royalty, or with any of the English. Not after what they had done to his forebears. He hasn't forgotten how they killed thousands of women and children in the concentration camps. Nor the black troups used against his people. Brutes, the Brits, when you came right down to it. But still.

He began to dream about them, both of them. Nothing nasty, at first; that came later. Sometimes, if he saw the older one flirting with other men, he would dream she was on her knees, begging and crying.

He has been back to the pool many times since then. He has taken his own children with him there on Sundays, though he has a pool of his own at Crossways. It reminds him of that time in his life.

VIII

K ATE SITS IN AN ORANGE PLASTIC CHAIR beside a potted plant,
smelling the strong hospital smell, feeling nauseated and
exhausted. She has the sick ache behind her eyes. They have
been asked to wait a moment before entering the intensive
care unit.

Her mother sits beside her, shifting about restlessly. She is
not used to being kept waiting. She has always been a woman
of authority, even before she married Kate's father and became
wealthy and moved into the big house. As a child she bossed
her older sister and younger brother around, Dottie has told
her. She would flush the toilet while Dottie sat on it, terrifying
her, she said, because she believed a witch might emerge from
the waters and carry her away, the way one did the fourth
child, a boy, at birth.

"How is Dr. Marais?" Julia calls out now in her loud voice
to the startled nurse, when she enters the room. She has lost a
little hearing, complains of a buzzing in her ears, and speaks
too loudly at times. Like many people with money she doesn't
hesitate to express her opinions. Kate remembers her coming
to school and singing the hymns off-key and very loudly in

her big, wide-brimmed hats and kid gloves, with the mother-of-pearl buttons. She remembers her calling all her school friends by the wrong names.

She was often embarrassing to them as girls, holding forth about her voyages at dinner parties, after a few drinks, "Ah, Banff! Lake Louise!" she would sigh nostalgically to people who had never left the city of Johannesburg.

Now she reiterates her question impatiently, "Is he well?"

The nurse mumbles, "As well as can be expected." The young woman has moist, violet eyes. Her starched white cap trembles on the back of her head like a child's boat on a wavy, blond sea. Clearly, she is upset. Has she already fallen in love with him, as everyone else does? Kate wonders.

"Do they know how damaged his mind is?" Kate's mother asks bluntly. The nurse hesitates, saying these things are always so hard to ascertain, and that it remains to be seen just how damaged. He has regained consciousness after the accident but seems somewhat confused and disorientated. There is a fine fracture of the skull and some bleeding into the brain. There is always hope that with time, this will improve. She ushers them into his room.

The walls and the bed sheets are green, and there is a machine in the next room, which gives off a regular hissing noise. The young nurse in her spotlessly white, rubber-soled shoes lingers near the bedside discreetly, protectively, her hands smoothing down the sheet.

At first Kate cannot bring herself to look at Louis's face, afraid of what she might see. Instead, she studies his hands, lying on the green sheet, the strong, sure hands of a surgeon. She remembers Marion telling her how gifted he was. "Some of them are, and some aren't. It's not really what they know," she had said.

"Like translating," Kate added.

When she does look at him, he seems to be sleeping, or perhaps he is pretending. She thinks he looks younger than his forty-three years: the face smooth, untouched apparently, the fair skin still tanned, the chin sharp, cheekbones high. A handsome man. She remembers saying to her sister, "You always said you wanted to marry a handsome doctor."

Her mother takes his hand into her two small, beringed ones. She leans over him tenderly and whispers, "Now you just rest up and get better soon, Louis, and come home to us at Crossways. The children are waiting for you."

Louis's eyes flicker open for a moment and seem to be looking at her. Then they shut immediately. The sudden flash of almost yellow, Kate remembers, eyes the color of his hair, of sunlight, the same color as Deidre's.

"Sister," he mumbles.

"Yes, what is it? What can I do for you?" the young nurse, who is standing by the window, asks, startled. She comes over to him quickly and looks down at him and touches his damp forehead. He looks up at her with his yellow cat's eyes for a moment, but his eyes give no inkling of his thoughts or emotions.

Kate wonders if this is the first time he has called out for the nurse. Or was he calling for her? Does he even recognize her? She watches the nurse lift his limp wrist and take his pulse. She shakes her head. "You rest up now. Too much excitement for one afternoon," she says soothingly and pats his hand and glares at them. She obviously considers this visit an intrusion, which Kate can understand: all the perfume, the flashing rings, the swishing of the silk jersey skirts, the tapping of the high heels.

Kate stares at the eminent surgeon, lying there with his eyes shut, mumbling rubbish, and clutching onto the side of his bed, as if he were afraid he might fall to the floor. She wonders if he will ever be able to work again, to save lives. She wonders just how much he remembers about his accident. She wonders, too, what really happened.

She remembers coming to the hospital with her sister and seeing him stride down the corridor in his white coat and the younger doctors crowd behind him to ask questions. She can hear them calling out, "Dr. Marais!"

Her mother goes on talking to him, prattling about the garden, the spring flowers, the little ones. "They are all being so well-behaved. No trouble at all," she says. There is no distrust in her voice or even indifference now, only warmth and kindness which Kate feels her mother has not demonstrated toward her since she has been home.

She wonders how her mother can invite this man to live with her. Does she really intend to eat breakfast with him every morning? Or does she plan on vacating her own house and leaving him with his children?

She thinks of her mother's voice on the telephone, when she called to inform Kate of the tragedy. She told her what had happened without any preamble.

Kate said what everyone says at such a moment, "It's not possible."

Her mother had sounded in a rage when she snapped, "I'm afraid it is," and told her where the accident had taken place that night in the convertible silver Mercedes, her mother's wedding present to the young couple. "She must have been killed instantly," her mother said.

Kate has always felt the suffering of others difficult to bear. This feeling has often caused her to miss the call of distress, caused her, rather to flee. She left her suffering country after Sharpeville, left her sister before her marriage to Louis. She has never consented to marry her own lover. Her work, her translations, the life of her mind, have set her apart from others.

She remembers how, as a girl, she would dream of a cloistered garden, chanting voices, the soft sound of nuns' skirts brushing against the stone, stone arches, long shadows, light filtering through the blue of stained glass, and altogether the presence of something vague and wonderful that she could only call God. Her mother was always afraid she might run off and marry a missionary.

She remembers saying to the distinguished doctor she consulted in Paris for depression, "I just don't want to dwell on pain I can do nothing about; what I want is to translate books." He had looked at her and smiled and told her those things might not be compatible.

In the reception area her mother signs some papers. Louis's own parents are no longer alive, and the rest of the family returned to the Great Karoo almost immediately after the funeral, taking with them the food left over from the reception. They have carried off the *padkos*: the smoked salmon canapes and even the remains of the Champagne. None of them have much money. Her sister's money, surely, has been left to the three children?

Kate finds herself saying to her mother and her aunt, "He's lucky to be alive." She wonders what made her sister forget her seat belt that night and why her husband was so conveniently wearing his. The young nurse has spoken of bruises across his chest from the belt. Had the couple quarrelled that night, as she knows they did so often? A clear night, her mother said, with no rain, and no other car involved. Kate has a good idea of what the accountant wanted to tell her so urgently, though she is not sure she wants to hear it.

Dottie now drapes the shawl around her sister's shoulders solicitously. She asks, "Do you think he even recognized us, Jule?"

"I'm quite warm enough, thank you," Julia says, her diamond rings catching the gold evening light as she moves her hands impatiently. "I had the impression he knew exactly who we were and what you were saying," Kate says, but her mother does not seem to have heard.

IX

H E STARES AT THE GREEN WALLS of his room. The chrome tray on the windowsill, the potted plant, and the dustbin are all settling back into place. He can still smell the women's perfume. When the sister was there, beside his bed, things had tumbled around him. When he saw the same dark hair, except longer, the same high-headed walk, and heard the same voice, the room danced and rocked as if he were on a boat. He had to clutch onto the side of the bed.

The mother was talking about his return to the house. Is it possible that he could return there? Could he just walk in the door and say, "I'm back"? Who would stop him? He looks up at the nurse, who stands beside him, looking down tenderly. He grins at her: not much she would stop him from doing.

He remembers when he first went there. He could not believe it when he heard where Serge was going. How incredibly lucky he was. "You're not going to a party at the Kempdens'!"

"Yes I am," Serge said and grinned.

Louis couldn't believe his friend, a fellow medical student, had been invited to their place. "Take me with you, please," he begged. Serge laughed and told him he couldn't just take him along. It wasn't that sort of invitation. It was only because his mother knew the aunt, and, anyway, why did he want to go so badly?

But Louis could be very persuasive like his father. He had been very persuasive with Pottie, the night he had been invited to celebrate his scholarship. He sat beside him on the old leather couch after dinner. Pottie had let him drink a beer or two. He had given him a thick steak. He had cooked it himself on the grill, without sugar or ash. He had served it underdone, not cooked into leather. Then things developed naturally.

He had managed to persuade Serge in a similar fashion. He told him it would be good for him, after what had happened to the old lady. Her big blue eyes were fixed on him. He thought of her as old, though she was probably not much more than fifty-five. He can still see the white hair, the big, pleading eyes. They had talked about her work. She was a schoolteacher, taught botany. She lived alone. They had discussed plants. She was interested in orchids. Then something went wrong. It was the first time. Heart gave out when he passed the tube down her throat. She made a little sound at the back of the throat, and she was gone. Bad things are inevitable, of course, when you are learning.

So Serge consented. He helped him rent the tuxedo. He even chipped in, though the only one they could afford was too tight. How it cut him under the arms and in the crotch.

He saw the house for the first time in the heavy rain. The alley of jacarandas dripped. The branches of the seringa tree in the driveway bent down under the onslaught of water. All the cars glistened. The flowers, one blue, one pink, drooped on either side of the Dutch front door. He heard the water gushing over the wall into the pool, the slamming of car doors, and the laughter on the lawn. Girls dashed for the door, giggling in their high heels.

The vast rooms dazzled him. The light colors of the walls and the shining silver blinded him: the oval, silver-framed photographs of the mother, the two girls as small children, their arms around one another, holding up a flower. The tall Zulu servant, who passed around the canapés in his starched white uniform with the blue sash over one shoulder and the tassel at the waist, dazzled him. He was astonished by the shining Steinway piano, open, waiting to be played. He had never seen a baby grand, only the old, battered upright with the plant on the top at Pottie's house, where he had learned to play in the hot afternoons. Pottie would stand behind him, lean over him, and put his fingers over his on the keys. He smelled of smoke, like Louis's mother. This, however, was something else. Louis had never seen anything like this.

Lekker, man, he had thought.

There was the shock of the two of them actually coming down the stairs together. The younger one, in a black dress, of all things, held the older one's hand. Or perhaps she had her arm around her waist, in that way they had. The older one wore a deep blue dress, with a full net skirt. He can see her so clearly. She was beating out a little rhythm with her narrow wrist on the bannister. The sisters were eyeing one another. They giggled. They were sharing some secret joke. The older one was humming some opera tune, in Italian, *nog*!

As he had at the public pool, he immediately felt excluded by their walk, their English accent, their closeness. He felt shut out by the way they seemed to understand one another with just a glance. They conspired like twins. He has never had that closeness with anyone. What would such a feeling be like?

They must have been nineteen and seventeen years old. It was 1958 perhaps? He cannot remember anymore. It was shortly after he had finished his qualifying exams. He could call himself a doctor now. He had done it all in record time, skipping a year. A phenomenon, his teachers had said. That made a real difference. If it hadn't been for the degree, the honors, he would never have dared to get Serge to take him along that night.

He remembers the doctor in the small town where he had grown up. A Jewish man with a shock of white hair and a prominent nose, he spoke good Afrikaans. He was the only one in the town with anything approaching an education. He was someone to look up to, unlike his father, who spent his time guzzling Castle beer at the local hotel, or his mother screaming for the bedpan.

"Such a strange, strange flutter," the aunt said about her heart, which had been giving her trouble. The disadvantage of a medical degree is that they are always coming at you with their symptoms.

"It might mean many things," he had replied, evasively. He wanted to get rid of her. He stared at the two girls. They stood with their arms around one another's waist at the foot of the stairs. They hovered on the edge of their party, as if it were someone else's.

In the background, he heard the murmur of voices muffled by heavy rain. He heard the water falling over the brick wall into the pool. He smelled the flowers.

"I used to be such a strong woman," the aunt explained breathlessly to him and Serge, "but ever since I turned fifty I have been falling apart. I am cracking up." She was trying to make a little joke. She was attempting to put him at ease, no doubt. He felt it must be obvious to everyone that he wasn't used to mixing with people from this background. He was certain everyone could see he was out of his depth in his tight rented tuxedo. The bow tie was strangling his neck. He regretted ever coming here. He regretted ever thinking he could say a word to these people, snooty English who talked as though they had hot potatoes in their mouths. He had aimed to enter a world above his station. What was he imagining?

He felt a wave of loneliness, envy, and anger. It was the largeness and the whiteness of the rooms, the lightness of the silk on the sofas, the brilliance of the silver. It was the unfairness of it all. He was afraid he would betray himself by dirtying all of this in some way.

The mother stood there with that smooth, creamy skin. She had luminous, hazel eyes. Her black crepe dress clung to her body. Her thick glossy hair was swept back from her face in an elaborate chignon, studded with pearls and diamonds. When she finally noticed her girls at her side in that crowded room, she gathered them together. She released a wave of strong scent as she introduced them to him, "My dear girls, I want you to meet Dr.—"

She pressed her hands against their backs, but she hesitated over his name. She thrust them both toward him like a gift or a bouquet, a double offering for the doctor. Two lilies, you might have said, but she got his name all wrong.

Lying there in his hospital bed, he realizes she has never really thought of him as a person. Afrikaners, to her, are not people, but brutes with hair on their backs. She makes fun of their accents. She ridicules their language which she cannot speak. She laughs at Afrikaans translations of the bible: "*Maak vas jou broek*," for "gird up your loins." This is supposed to be hilarious. She thinks they all live in houses with dirt floors and commit incest on their isolated farms. In her ignorance she thinks they have no culture, no proverbs, no stories, no history, no poetry. He has heard the sort of things she has said in her ignorant, loud voice. He was never more than an appendage, a useful one, at best a purveyor of pills, a producer of babies, the father of her grandchildren, a nurse, or what she probably now needs, a nanny.

But at that party, he didn't yet know all of that, he just thought she had forgotten his name. He corrected her. He shook Marion's hand. He did not dare look down at her breasts, but he glimpsed the pendant which hung between them. Three diamonds, one bigger than the next, dangled there. He was looking at the younger girl in her dark dress, too.

"The doctor worked in a team with Christian Barnard," the mother informed her girls.

They said nothing to that. Not impressed, he could see, only a little laugh, trapped in the bitten lower lips.

The aunt said, "Our young doctor has done so much already for my palpitations." She batted her eyelashes at him. She fingered the lace at the neck of her dress.

The mother smiled at him graciously and said, "Indeed, I'm sure Dr. Marais could do us all good."

"Perhaps," Marion said and offered him a half-smile. She was almost as tall as he.

The younger one, too, glanced up at him.

It all seemed suddenly so easy. He felt a sudden shift in his mood, a buoyant lift of his heart. He noticed the differences between the girls. The older one was softer, more supple. Her glossy hair curled about her lovely face. He wanted to tell her he had seen her at the pool. He wanted to confess he had fallen in love, no, into adoration. He wanted to tell everyone he adored her, that she shone with a halo. She glowed for him. He wanted to blurt it out. He wanted to write it up in the newspaper, announce it over a loudspeaker, carve it into a tree: LOUIS MARAIS ADORES MARION KEMPDEN.

He was already imagining their life together. He saw the doors opening before him. He imagined the people smiling, bowing, looking up to him, with a wife like that on his arm. He thought of how all the other blokes would be envious of him, green with envy. That made him smile. He thought how no one, no one, would dare call him what he had been called when they found him with another boy in the locker room at school: *moffie*.

He knows he is not like men of that kind. He likes women, Goddamn it. Certain women. He likes the big-boned, quiet ones, who don't come on too strong. He likes placid women, with a little dark hair on the upper lip.

He remembers the moment, with that boy now. He lies in his hospital bed and closes his eyes. He feels the longing rushing into his limbs. He runs his hands across the boy's narrow chest, the dark-haired boy with dusky skin who was no good at math. They had been mock-fighting in the locker room, rolling around on the concrete floor, laughing. He had him pinned. "Let me go," he said. Louis could smell his hair, his damp skin, his boy-smell. He pressed his shoulders and grabbed the coarse hair. He rubbed his body against him. He felt a sudden burst of happiness. Then the door opened, and he saw the grinning faces and heard the dreadful mocking laughter, *moffie, moffie, moffie*. The shame of it. He learned early in his life that there are things it is best not to think about, that even shame passes if you don't let yourself dwell on it.

With Marion no one would laugh at him. No one would call him names.

X

SOMETIMES JOHN LONGS TO LEAVE THIS HOUSE of many clocks which is not his own, though he has lived here longer and knows all its secrets better than anyone else.

He knows how Hans Kempden's first wife was killed in a motor car accident, strangled by her own scarf somehow while out for a drive with him, after he had divorced her and had married the beautiful housekeeper, Julia, with the small hands and feet. He has seen the ghost of the first Mrs. Kempden on the stairs, where she walks up and down, the stairs that he has kept so impeccably polished and dusted all these years. He has seen her ghost try to pull the pink gauze scarf from her throat.

He remembers coming up for the first time to *eGoli*, his people's name for Johannesburg, as a boy and how amazed he was to see the wide tarmac roads, the stores, the traffic lights, the post office, the bank, the secondary school, the motor cars, the well-tended flowers and shrubs. He took his new shoes off and spread his toes on the smooth tarmac and walked down the road staring in wonder.

As a boy he would never have spoken to his elders the way the children do today. By the time he was five or six he already knew how to be useful and productive. He was brought up to obey the laws of his people blindly and absolutely, just like Shaka's *impis*, who, when ordered to walk off a cliff, walked to their deaths without murmuring. But the young ones no longer listen to the old stories or the laws of his people, and they probably don't even know the names of Shaka's half brothers: Dingana, Mbopa, and Mhlangana, or who the tyrant Shaka himself was or even Dingi-Swayo, the inventor of the short stabbing spear, which brought so many victories to his people. They have never heard of Islandlwana, the battleground where his people defeated so many white men.

These young ones know nothing about their history, and without tradition and law, how can people live? All they want is to listen to their rubbish music and drink *skokiaan* and shout at one another and swear. Sometimes he thinks they are all mad.

He longs to go back to his homeland and his own people and walk into his *kraal*, a village of seven or eight huts, and lay down his head on the smooth, worn, cow-dung floor. He has not been back for a long while, and he has not asked for any holiday leave. He cannot imagine what the *Nkosi* would do in his absence, and how she could run this big house and garden without his help, without him to make sure that the other servants did their work properly, and to perform the rituals that protected the house from evil spirits.

On his Thursday afternoon off, he takes a walk and goes toward the city or just lies under a tree with his gray hat tipped over his face, dozing, or crouches down with his back to the wall, smoking his pipe in the sun.

He doesn't go to any of the Christian churches many of the other servants attend on Sunday afternoons, when they dress up in blue robes and sing and shout and dance and bow their heads in humiliation or get themselves in a froth over nothing at all. Like Julia Kempden, John believes much of that is what she calls "baloney." "A bunch of bible-punching hypocrites," she likes to say to him, and he laughs and nods his head, when the proselytizers come to the door to leave their literature, or when the minister from the church visits with his wife in her hat with the trembling flowers and the long gloves to drink a glass of sherry and to lure his *Nkosi* and her money to his church.

He believes in the spirit of his ancestors. He thinks of his life of labor as a connection between his ancestors and his only remaining child and the children he still hopes she will have, though she is nearing the age when children are no longer possible, and he fears she will remain barren. When worried, he thinks of his warrior ancestors marching bravely into battle, singing their battle songs, and though he cannot sing very well, he whistles under his breath to keep up his courage.

The other servants don't say much to him, and he knows they think he is out of date, a self-righteous prude and a snob, but he is used to solitude. They only talk to him when it is necessary, for they know he has a privileged place in this house, that he is the one the *Nkosi* prefers to them, that she trusts him completely with the keys, and all her secrets. She confides her troubles and her joys to him alone, he believes. The other servants only come to him when they need his help or want to get something out of him, but he refuses to lend them his hard-earned money or allow them to bring their relatives to sleep in his small room, and he has little to say to them except for the counsel he would give them if they would listen.

When he goes home, he is obliged to take the crowded train, with his whole year's salary hidden in his socks. He saves all his money, for his food and his uniforms and his Lifebuoy soap are all given to him, and sometimes the *baas* gives him a good suit or a sweater, whose tatters he darns carefully when they appear. He spends only a few pennies on tobacco for his pipe, his only luxury. He has always been a thrifty man, and he buys only the essentials.

He is always careful not to fall asleep on the train, but years ago on his voyage home with his entire year's salary in his socks, he was set upon by *tsotsis*, despite his vigilance. He saw the two heavy-set men who sat opposite him in the compartment watching him. They wore shiny suits and fancy shoes with tassels, and he knew they meant trouble when the one brought out a roll of sweets and offered him one, smiling and showing good teeth, one of them flashing gold. John shook his head at the sweets, but when he rose for a necessity, they followed him and caught him in the corridor, where they came up behind him like cowards and hit him over the head. He fell to the floor, and they kicked him in the ribs, and broke two of them. They slashed at his arm with a knife, when he raised it to defend himself, as his ancestors would have done, and they would probably have killed him had not someone come down the corridor. As it was, they ran off with all his hard-earned money and his shoes, which were new ones and well-polished, just that morning, and no one else knows how to polish shoes the way he does. They left him lying there, stunned, bleeding, half-dead, and bare-footed, with nothing left to take to his wives.

Surrounded now by dim forms, the only things he sees very clearly are the images in his memory. He sees all the ghosts of his past, and the ravages of the earth. He sees his village as it was when he was a boy: the ochre-colored landscape and the thin herd-boys, sticks in hand, standing on the barren, over-grazed hills. They looked after cattle whose ribs you could count. Brightly colored birds swooped down to catch black beetles rolling dung up the slopes, and streams flowed feebly in the summer rains, dying in the winter drought, and round thatched-roofed huts huddled in groups of three or four. The door to the four-walled tin-roofed building, belonging to the blacksmith banged against its frame, and his mother sat before a hut and sifted flour to knead into bread.

He wishes he could leave Crossways and go back to his homeland, but there are the dangerous trains, and his only remaining child, Ellen, does not welcome his return. She is an educated woman, who teaches school and calls him a country bumpkin, because to his shame he has never learned to read or write, nor does he know his age, though he knows he is very old, for he feels it in his aching bones and in the irregular flutter of his heart. She does not understand that he has something much better than a whole library of books in his head, for his memories can never be taken from him, and they contain the stories his tribe tells and the history of his people, which she used to love to hear. Does she not understand that he has taught her many things with his stories about good and evil, about sagacity and quick wits, about courage and truth?

She makes him sit in the kitchen and drink his tea like a servant in her house from a tin mug, which burns his lips, and she does not tell him what is in her heart. He would like to leave this house of sorrows, where he has lived and worked for so long but he has many essential duties to accomplish here. The wishes of the dead must be respected.

XI

KATE HEARS THE TELEPHONE RINGING in the night. She stumbles down the stairs in her sister's pink silk gown.

"Who is it?" she asks. She stands at the bottom of the stairs in the dimly lit hall, the belt tied tightly around her waist. She curls her long toes on the cold parquet. She has narrow, white feet. Kate is not as tall as her sister was.

Rene has called her in the middle of the night to ask when she is coming home. "I'm going crazy without you. I cannot write, cannot eat, cannot stand it," he says. Rene, so obsure in his work, is dreadfully direct in his conversation.

She imagines him lying at the bottom of the pool where they sometimes go together, his long, dark hair floating around him. But surely, if he can tolerate the abstemious Lacan, he can bear her absence for a few weeks? He has been doing an analysis with Jacques Lacan for years and reports that Lacan frequently asks him to leave the session after he has voiced only one or two sentences.

"Wednesday night. I'll try to be back by Wednesday night," she promises, standing beneath the stairs in the shadowy hall at one in the morning.

But Wednesday night comes and goes and then another Wednesday night.

Her translation of Rene's poetry is not one of which she is particularly proud. There were too many obscure references, too many leaps and bounds, too many puns and plays on words she had not really understood. She is not good at puns and wordplays, and when she asked for clarifications from him, they only confused her further, and she found herself drifting off into her own thoughts.

The critics, however, liked the difficult book. They liked the darkness, the silences, what they called the "attention that points to a religious sensibility," though she knows that he is not religious at all. The *Times Literary Supplement* called her translation "elegant," and the *New York Times* called the book, published in America by a prestigious house, "a thing of beauty, full of riddles and undergirded with deep, dark layers of philosophical meditation."

After that she was suddenly inundated with requests to translate difficult texts by writers such as Barthes and Bachelard, Derrida, Robbe-Grillet and even Foucault. Despite all the praise, which included a prestigious prize, and the considerable sum of money its author received, she sometimes wonders now if Rene himself knew what his sentences meant. In any case she is afraid she has rendered them no less incomprehensible.

Still, he has been trying to persuade her to marry him for years. He does not seem threatened by her success as a translator of others' texts. He wants her to leave Paris with him and settle in an old farmhouse he bought with his prize money in the hills near Saint Paul de Vence, surrounded by vineyards. She finds this intensity frightening, as she does at times when he takes her into his arms, presses her against his thin body, and trembles. She is always afraid she will not be able to respond adequately. She is also afraid of losing the only thing she has, her work, if she gives in completely.

XII

HE WANTED TO ESCAPE THE AUNT, who was gushing all over him, and all the other guests, and the heat in the room. He wanted to be alone with the older sister. He suggested that they go out into the garden on the night of the party, even though it was raining gently.

She stared at him for a moment, as if she had not quite understood. She asked in her drowsy voice, "Into the rain?" But to his surprise, she did not resist. She let him lead her across the misty lawn. She had that way of walking, that seemed like drifting.

They huddled under one of the jacaranda trees. Trembling, he held the jacket of his rented tux over her head to protect her from the rain. He prayed it would not be ruined, a month's salary wasted. He could smell the wetness of the grass, the material, and her skin.

She stood there, not responding, probably thinking about something else. Perhaps she, too, simply wanted to escape the crowd. She wasn't giggling or silly, the way girls often were. She hardly seemed to notice him. Her neck was soft, and she smelled nice, like ripe fruit. He nuzzled into her smell. She didn't seem to care. He could hear her soft breathing, feel the warm air of her breath, and the heat from her plump, soft, steamy body. He was trembling a little, like a stallion, and aroused like one, too. He wasn't pressing his body up against her; he didn't dare. But she didn't struggle when he put his arm around her shoulder gently and contained her.

He whispered something into her ear about having seen her dive at the public pool. He told her how she almost hit her head. He was holding her, yet he felt as if it were happening to someone else. He had no desire to close his eyes or swoon like a girl. He wanted to see this all happen, as if he were watching in a mirror.

The whole, elaborate party with the flowers and the rich dessert and the jewels was unreal. He had difficulty believing it had really happened. All those boring people, talking nonsense with their English accents, and that tall Zulu with his blue tassel were unreal. The mother with the diamonds like drops of rain in her hair was more real than anyone else. He could have gone for her. Or for the younger sister, standing there in her dark dress like the older one's shadow. She would have done just as well.

But he was out in that misty garden with this one. The rain had stopped. She seemed uninterested in what he was doing. He dropped the jacket. The trees dripped. The moths hovered. The damp, light-blue flowers dipped down low over the brick walls. Her dress was the same color as the flowers. The waterfall splashed faintly. They were out in the garden where anyone could see them, exposed.

He heard muffled, strange voices come across the lawn, the mother's warm, throaty laugh, the sounds of the servants in the kitchen, someone swearing in Zulu. He listened to her little, polite protests, finally, and her bored voice. They excited him. She didn't care if he did or he didn't.

In the distance, silhouetted by the lights from the grand house, he could see some bloke walking across the lawn, as if in slow motion. He turned his head to look at him. Louis could see the glow of his cigarette. The stranger's presence in the garden was not embarrassing; it excited him. Afterwards, he thought that, had that bloke not wandered out into the garden, at that moment, had he not stopped quite still and turned his head toward them, had Louis not felt his eyes watching them, nothing would have happened. He would have let the girl slip from his grasp, which she was trying to do.

"Let me go, will you," she said, without much conviction.

He said, "But this is what you want, isn't it?"

He had her, a big girl, almost as tall as he, with her swimmer's shoulders, her long, strong legs, her diamonds, her blue dress with the full skirt, pressed up against the tree. He thrust up against her now. He saw her back arch. She threw back her head. He saw his hands slide down to her buttocks. She pressed up against him. She gave up, completely. She abandoned herself.

There was the soft dripping from the leaves on his face. His mouth and hers were damp. He saw himself slip his hand down the v-neck of her blue dress. He bent down and sucked at her nipple. He put his hand up her plump thigh and felt the warmth and the melting between her legs. She opened up. In the intermittent light of the moon and the lights from the house he could see her face. There was an expression of total abandonment in her closing eyes. Her lips were parted, and she was smiling, he was certain.

She had her back against the old tree, one of those familiar jacarandas. His leg was between hers. He pressed as if his life depended on it. He felt nothing could stop him now. He had felt this before. He was caught up by something strong and irresistible. It moved him and made him all-powerful. He saw doors opening before him.

Before he had time to think about it, he had her full skirt up. Her pants came down easily. He saw his hands lifting her rounded cheeks. He opened them up a bit. He was in her soft flesh, wet like the rain in her hair, the diamonds between her breasts, those in her mother's hair.

He felt something warm and soft pressed against his flesh, something that made him feel a surge of joy, desire, and power. Then, with a jolt, something gave way to him. He was inside her and swelling. He was swooping down from the sky, disturbing the air around her with a great clashing of wings, catching her up in his claws, and lifting her up again. He carried her off through the air. There was no stopping him. He left himself behind.

It was quick. He hadn't ever had an orgasm inside a woman like that. He was defying death, fucking his way out of the grave. The old woman's blue eyes were open and her dying gaze was on him.

There was no blood, no cry, no dramatic protestation. She became perfectly quiet. She watched him with her eyes open and blank.

The bloke, too, was watching from across the lawn. The cigarette still burned in his hand.

XIII

J OHN LIES ON HIS NARROW COT against the cement wall in his small, smoky room in the servants' quarters. It is very late, nearly morning by now, and he has finished his work some time ago, but sleep, which he thinks of as the "little death," does not come for him, and his spirit is not set free to wander, though his old bones ache with fatigue and he feels cold, even this warm spring night, and he has eaten his dinner, and lies under his thick, striped blanket. He often feels cold these days, lying alone in his cot, and he senses that the food he eats does not nourish him, and does not stick to his bones. He fears what may lie up ahead in this house, now that his *Kskatie* has come home. He knows she has been with her mother and her aunt to visit the *baas*, who is lying in his bed in the hospital with damage to his head. John is sorry he cannot take him to see the witch doctor he knew in his homeland.

She is a clever one, that one. On his last visit to his homeland one of his wives, the youngest, the cheekiest, who is always asking him for money, suggested he consult her for his failing sight. "She will cure you," his wife maintained with the optimism of her younger years. So he consented, to please her, and to see for himself whether this one knew how to throw the bones the way the old ones did.

When he entered the woman's cave, he could hardly see, and he looked for her in the faint light cast by the sticks of incense, which he could smell burning in a corner. She was sitting with her back to him, cross-legged, head half-bowed and arms outstretched, on a reed mat on the ground. On the walls of her cave he made out the usual bones and skins of wild animals and bark and roots of different plants, though he could not see clearly enough to name them. There were bottles of liquids with pungent smells.

Then she turned her head and greeted him with the traditional greeting, and he saw she had yellow mud caked on her face and what seemed to be a goat's bladder tied to the end of one of her strands of hair.

He wanted to test her ability, for he was not sure that she was up to the difficult task. He asked her first to tell him about his life, before he allowed her to cure him. She told him all about his life with such precise details that certain things he had forgotten from his childhood came back to him, and he was amazed. She divined that he had once fallen while running when one of the other children had banged into him, going down a hill, causing him to pull something in his leg which had never healed completely.

Then he asked her to give him some *muti* for his failing sight, and she took up the bones and the shells and slowly shook them in her knobby hands and threw them onto the mat, staring at them for a long while, as though she were in a trance. She shook her head and warned him that the other servants in the house were envious of him, because of his favored position with his *Nkosi*, so much so that they would have killed him if his ancestors had not protected him. All they could do was to cast this spell on him to render him blind, hindering him in his work, in order to cause his downfall and removal from the big house. She said there was no *muti* she could give him to help him to regain his sight, but she could tell him what he must do.

He listened.

She advised him to leave the house immediately and to come back home to his remaining wives and to rest here in his homeland; then he would gradually regain his sight. But he shook his head and told her he was not able to do such a thing, that he could not desert his *Nkosi* who had such a great need of his help, that he was obliged to organize her household and ward off the evil spirits with the chicken blood, which he spills on the ground twice a year. She shook her head and predicted many sorrows for him and for the family where he abided, and he knows now that she spoke truly.

He feels a draft around his head, hears a familiar sound, and looks up, thinking it might be *Kskatie* who has come looking for him, to talk to him as she would do sometimes in the night as a girl, when she could not sleep. But his door is closed, and there is no window, and although it is still dark at this hour, he sees Miss Marion's ghost quite clearly, as it walks toward the end of his bed, wearing the pink and white bracelet and pink silk nightgown, the one she brought back from her visit to Rome. It is making the sound she sometimes made by sucking on her teeth, and its feet are bare, and the hem of its gown, which trails behind it, is dusty, and its face is caked with yellow mud, like the face of the witch doctor.

But the ghost does not speak to him as the witch doctor did: it only stands at the end of his bed and turns its head and blinks large, dark eyes and looks at him in silence for a moment as it has done before. This time he notices that it is holding a letter in its hand. It walks slowly over to his white suit, the good one which he wears to serve at table with the blue or the red sash, which goes from one shoulder to his tasseled waist. He washed the suit that morning with cold water and starch and ironed it himself and hung it up behind the door, because he does not trust anyone else to do it properly. The ghost slips the letter into the pocket of the jacket and turns and drifts toward the door.

When he calls out to it to wait, to speak to him, to tell him what he must do with the letter, it lifts a hand as if it were about to say something to him, but he hears the cock crow, and it leaves him as suddenly as it had appeared, and he does not even have the time to tell it, *hamba kahle*, and he falls into a heavy, deep sleep as though drugged.

At first, when he awakes, he thinks he might have dreamed this visitation of the early morning, because he knows old men often believe they lie awake all night, while they are only snoring away in their beds, but when he rises and puts his hand into the pocket of his jacket, he finds the letter there. He understands what the ghost wishes him to do to protect its sister and the children it has left behind in his care.

XIV

T HERE IS THE QUESTION of what to do with the children. What would be the best thing for them? Kate asks her mother and aunt this November afternoon. They glance at one another but go on with their knitting, clicking their steel needles fast, sitting side-by-side on the silk-covered sofa in the lounge, slim legs in pale nylon stockings held to one side and crossed at the fine ankles, cream pleated skirts arranged decorously.

She looks out the window, where the children are playing tea party on the trestletable, watched over by John under the oak tree in the late afternoon light. She wonders if they are using the acorns for cups, as she and her sister did.

She suggests that her mother and aunt might well want to take care of the children themselves, now that their mother has been so cruelly and abruptly taken from them. They would have plenty of help, after all, with John there and the rest of the servants.

"And they would be company for you," she says cheerfully.

Her mother puts down her knitting and takes a gulp of her whiskey and soda.

"We are not lonely, you know," Dottie replies, continuing to beat her needles back and forth rapidly, and she thinks she catches a fierce glare of disapproval in her aunt's small, dark eyes, as if she were saying, "What on earth are you thinking! At our age!"

It would be Dottie, obviously, the poor relation, who at sixty-three, would have to do much of the onerous work, rising in the night in case of sickness or sorrow, being called upon to go and see teachers, doctors, that sort of thing. Kate understands that her suggestion is not welcomed. Dottie has taken care of Julia with much devotion, but there are limits.

"Then I will stay for as long as necessary," Kate says. She has been out here for three weeks now. Rene has continued to call. He is increasingly impatient and anxious. "I'm falling apart," he keeps saying.

"You are spending too much money on these calls," she says, but she thinks of her three shady, cool rooms in Paris, her bookcases along one wall with her dictionaries, the elegant Louis Quinze desk where she works, the one her mother bought for her on one of her visits to Paris. She thinks of her work, the juggling she does with words. She would prefer to go back.

She feels different when she speaks a different language. She was a different child speaking Zulu, one who felt free to speak her mind, wild and fierce, who danced half-naked in the rain, ran around barefoot in the mud, climbed trees, decked herself with flowers, and slept in the sun.

She remembers how she and her sister would run out ecstatically into the driveway after rain and shake the branches of the jacaranda tree nearest the house and soak their clothes and dance wildly, twisting their hips back and forth and waving their arms around, the way they imagined the Zulu Gods might do.

Now she has become different, speaking French. Sometimes she feels more intelligent speaking French than English, as though the language itself, the complicated structure of the sentences, the precise grammar, has sharpened her discourse, clarified and ordered her thoughts. Sometimes she has to search for an English word.

She remembers speaking Zulu as a small child with John and her sister, and being obliged to become someone else when her mother sent them off to the world of the Anglican boarding school, soon after her father died, when she was eight years old. There she began to forget the language of her early days of freedom in the garden. She remembers lying in her lonely bed at night at boarding school, trying desperately to remember the lullaby John would sing to her and her sister in Zulu, as though, if she could not find the words, she would never be able to sleep again. Once, she had a terrible dream in which she saw John on the staircase and did not recognize him.

She thinks of the bakery on the corner of her street, of the butcher shop, the bookstore with its old books exposed in the flickering sunlight on the pavement under the plane trees. She remembers the wide square with the fountain and the church and the doves, the university across the park where she teaches a course on translation. She thinks of her young students, the dark-haired girl, with the little space between her two front teeth who follows her down the corridor and looks up at her with admiration.

She looks at the children, who are playing their game so quietly at the trestletable across the lawn. She imagines their good behavior as something new, more pronounced than on earlier visits.

The eldest child, Mark, wears his hair long so that it falls into his dark, solemn eyes. Gray rings circle them like ash, and his skin is as pale as milk. He is capable of the same kind of dreamy concentration as his mother at that age. His head is tilted forward with such a pitch of concentration, it frightens her. He sits bolt upright at the trestletable, as though watching over his sisters.

There are times when he suddenly speaks up, startling her. He has told her a story about the silkworms he keeps in a cardboard shoebox which he has poked holes into with his pencil, to give them air. They rustle around in there, silvery fat little creatures, eating away at the mulberry leaves. "They eat and eat," he has told her.

Lydia wears her brown hair as Kate did as a girl, in tight plaits with big bows fluttering at the ends. She strokes Kate's skirt, the touch as soft as a fledgling's wing, saying, "I like your dress."

At five, she is lighter eyed, thinner and fiercer than her brother. She has her mother's thick, dark lashes and small, plum-colored mouth. She touches Kate's stockings, letting her hand slide gently on her knee, looking up at her admiringly. The terrible thing is her admiration is sincere. There is so much hope in her gray eyes, Kate feels she can only disappoint.

No disappointment can come to the white-haired baby, who still regards Kate with suspicion from her slanting cat's eyes, clinging to her big brother or to John if Kate approaches.

She looks at the lawn, still brown from the long winter drought, and listens to the sad call of the turtledove in a bluegum tree. She smells the bitter odor of burning compost.

She remembers thinking, when she matriculated, "Either you leave this country or you go to jail."

She looks out the window and watches the children play their game in the twilight. John rises and takes the little one by the hand, the way he taught her sister to hold hers.

XV

AGAIN, SHE RUNS DOWN THE STAIRS to answer the phone in the night.

"Hallo, hallo," she says, but, this time, no one responds. "Who is this?" she asks. She hears only breathing on the other end. She stands in the hall repeating hallo, remembering how people said her voice sounded exactly like her sister's.

Her sister was simply there from the beginning: they were inseparable. She grasped her hand, her arm, her fingers, put them in her mouth. They sucked one another's thumbs. She clambered across Marion's pale child chest, thumped her stomach, and scratched in her navel. She lay her head down between her legs, touched her *gnomie*, the little man who lived in there. Marion wanted her to.

They lay head to head in the sunlight on the concrete at the side of the swimming pool, striped towels over their backs and touched the tips of their tongues together and giggled; a bee stung one of them while they were touching tongues—Kate doesn't remember which one it was, and their mother told them that's what happened to naughty girls.

They could never go swimming until three hours after lunch or they would get cramps and drown. They wore the same green water wings, and the identical swimming costumes their mother and aunt had knitted with their initials embroidered on the breast. They stood side by side on the concrete, their tummies swelling with all the boiled vegetables, mutton and caper sauce. Their arms formed a V as they held hands tightly, jumping into the water. Kate followed her up and down the pool, dog-paddling behind her as fast as she could, the water her sister kicked up splashing her face. She tried to remain in the water, her lips blue, her teeth chattering.

When they were told to get out, they tied string around their dolls and dragged them around the pool, teaching them how to swim on their backs, but the dolls flipped over and fell face-down.

They went down into the bottom of the garden, where the wild grass and the bamboo grew. It was a different world there. They crossed the stile, which led from the smooth lawns to the wild acres of long grass and black jacks and bamboo, where they played their secret games. The stile had to be climbed backwards, one step at a time, so that they would be safe from the *Tokolosh* who lurked there.

They played their favorite game, "doll," down there. One of them had to lie completely still, flat on her back, looking up at the waving bamboo, unblinking, arms at her side. The other gave the orders. She had to do exactly as she was told, lift her legs in the air, and put her hand between them.

They played "my dears," lifting their little fingers in the air and pretending to be their mother and Dottie, taking tea on the veranda, saying "My dear, if you only knew!"

"Let's go back to the house and ask John for a Coke," Marion said, and took her hand. They trudged slowly back up the bank and through the servants' courtyard and into the kitchen. She sat beside her sister on the lawn in the shade and sipped her Coke carefully, looking to see how much Marion had left in her bottle, making sure she sipped hers just as slowly. She was the echo, the stutter in her sister's words. She tried to be exactly the same as her sister, but she always fell just short.

XVI

THE NURSE LEANS OVER HIS BED. She pats the back of his hand. He has a sudden, strong urge to smack her across her pretty face with it.

It is the same urge he had when his wife would ask him what he was doing. Her tone sounded exactly like his mother's accusatory one, when she interrupted his private activity. But he lets this nurse go on patting his hand. She can't keep hers off him.

He mumbles "Crossways," to this nurse with the moist, violet eyes. He remembers the rain that night. He is not certain anymore how much is real confusion and how much is acting. Mostly, he exaggerates, dressing up the truth.

Serge has told him, "Use as much truth as you can, if you want to lie." That is what he is doing, so well, he hardly knows any longer what really happened.

He knows his wife is dead. He knows his children are alone in the house with the grandmother, the great aunt, and K.K. He has called the house a few times just to hear the sound of her familiar voice. He wants to see her again. He wonders what her lonely life in Paris is doing for her, after all. Her face looked pale, and she has grown a bit thin. He could put some color back into her cheeks.

No one seems to be bothering him much now. Dr. Walsh has given up, or given in. It wasn't hard to outwit him, the bloody psychiatrist! He has not had many visits since the in-laws came, not even from Serge. He would like to see him. Serge must know what has happened to him. Serge knows everything.

He says, "I would like to go home for my birthday," and watches the nurse frown. Is it disappointment? Surely she is supposed to be pleased by this sign of progress.

The girl is too young for the job, he thinks. If he were the doctor in charge on this ward, he would do something about this girl. In her innocence and self-absorbtion, she is likely to cause trouble.

"Next Sunday," he says, though he realizes she can probably find out it is not his birthday at all, not his birthday for months. "I want to go home and be with my children for my birthday."

As he speaks, things becomes vivid. He imagines the driveway, the alley of jacarandas, the Dutch door with the blue and pink flowers on either side, the hall, the curving bannister, the green carpet on the stairway which leads upstairs to the bedrooms.

XVII

THAT MORNING HER SISTER DIDN'T WANT HER ON HER BED. She didn't even want her to touch her bed. Please don't touch my bed! Marion sat on the edge of her bed in her long white viyella nightdress sipping her glass of passion fruit juice, her bare calves and feet dangling. Kate sat on the edge of her bed in her identical nightdress, leaned over, and touched her sister's bed.

"Don't touch my bed!" her sister said again and lifted up her hand, her fingers spread like a hedge.

She reached out again and touched her bed fast. "I told you. Don't touch my bed!" her sister screamed, her face red, and Kate did it again. Marion turned puce and her lips trembled with rage. She picked up her glass and threw her passion fruit juice all over Kate's clean white nightdress. She screamed.

Screaming, Kate ran down the long corridor, her sister following across the landing. In the muted light of the mauve bedroom with the double curtains closed on the early morning sunlight, her mother lay in the big bed under the silk counterpane. Without her red lipstick which she smeared on cups, glasses, and napkins, her face was so pale it looked masked in its nakedness against the blue pillows.

"Why on earth are you screaming like that?" her mother asked her.

Because I spilled my juice," her sister explained.

"Spilled juice on me," Kate blubbered.

"For goodness sake. Come here to Mummy," their mother said and opened up her arms to Kate. Her mother removed her wet nightdress and took her into her bed to comfort her, while Marion sat on the stool before her dressing table, banging her heels against its legs.

Then her mother tucked her into the bed beside her, covered her over with the blue sheet, and sang to her. She turned to her mother and tilted up her chin to her, like a beak, and her mother pulled her transparent nylon nightdress aside and lifted out her soft, white breast. She offered Kate her thick, brown nipple to suck, stroking her dark curls. "Poor, poor pet," she said, "Poor, poor darling girl." Kate's eyes glazed over with pleasure, and she sucked hard and rhythmically, while twirling her mother's curls slowly through her fingers. She could hardly see her sister on the stool. Kate was somewhere else, somewhere lovely, but distant. She left her sister, willed herself away while her sister ate the anchovy toast cut into small squares on their mother's breakfast tray, kicked her heels against the stool, and scowled.

Her mother laughed and said to Marion, the first one, "You never liked to suck, did you?" Spitting out her tongue like a stone, she made a rude noise, to imitate the way Marion had refused her nipple.

XVIII

HER MOTHER HAS PUT HER in the small blue room, which is now used as a guest room, though she suspects her sister must have slept here at times and again recently. There are subtle signs of her presence, her faint perfume of verbena and lavender on the pillow. She lifts it and holds it against her nose and breathes deep.

She is woken in the night by the sound of crying in the room next door. It is Deidre. She rises and stumbles through the adjoining door in the blue light and tries to take the little one into her arms and rock her to sleep, but the child pushes her away, sitting upright against the wall, straight white hair falling into her face. She opens her big mouth wide and cries lustily for her "Mormie."

Kate fears a chorus of three desperate wailers, but the other two sleep on, as only small children can do, despite the racket. She gathers the child up, takes her into the blue room, and closes the door. She sits her on the bed. The child screams even louder, kicks her little legs in fury at this forced separation from her brother and sister.

She tries to sing her the old lullaby John used to sing for them and she begins "Lala..." but cannot remember the rest of the words. She even resorts guiltily to feeding her handfuls of the sweets she and her sister loved, *hopjes*, which she finds in the back of the bedside table drawer. For a moment or two, with her mouth full, liquid sugar trickling down her chin, the child stops screaming, and Kate holds her breath, hoping this is the end.

She cannot imagine how so small a child has found the energy, the desperation, to cry with such unrelenting force. She remembers her sister telling her how she had read in Dr. Spock that no child will cry for more than half an hour. Wrong! wrong! she thinks. Deidre will never stop.

"I wish your *Mormie* were here to take care of you," she says nastily, exasperated. Deidre pronounces the word, as if there were an "r" in it. Eventually, the child's white head falls forward, and she collapses against Kate, who gathers her up in her arms and slips her into the bed against the blue wall. She lies beside her, not daring to move, one arm dead with the weight of the child across it, through the night.

In the morning, her swollen eyes flicker open, and she glances up at Kate. There is a little smile on the tear-stained face, then she rubs her eyes and stares at Kate, frowning. Her lips tremble and turn down at the sides. She says, "I thought you were my *Mormie*," and begins to weep again. Kate carries her downstairs into the kitchen where, to her relief, she finds John already awake and boiling his porridge in the first light of day. She hands him the child, who stops weeping as soon as he lifts her onto his back. She puts her arms around his neck, nuzzles her face against his skin, hiccups, and sniffs.

Then Kate climbs back into her bed and sleeps. The sound of the water, running over the wall, finds its way into her sleep, hushing her body with its rhythm, carrying her back to the shallows of her memory.

XIX

O N THE MORNING THEIR FATHER DIED, Marion ran along the corridor from the nursery into the big mauve bedroom. The nurse took her by the shoulders and pushed her roughly out of the door, but not before she had seen their father lying there unmoving on the bed, the curtains closed, his skin gray, in the muffled light.

She ran back to Kate in the nursery to tell her what had happened, and Kate felt the nurse had grasped her, too, by the shoulders and pushed her roughly out of the door. Kate could feel the nurse's strong hands on her shoulders, the rudeness of being thrust out of the bedroom door so abruptly; she could hear the rustle of the white starched uniform, the squelch of the nurse's crepe-soled shoes. She, too, had seen their father lying there unmoving on the bed, dead, though she had seen nothing at all, except herself in the mirror, her round face and dark hair in tight plaits with the bows on the end. She stood before the mirror on the back of the closet door and decided she was supposed to cry. Her sister was at the door, tearless, watching her. She said, in her sensible way, "You don't have to cry, you know," so Kate didn't.

Then their Mother opened the door to the nursery. She was wearing a purple dressing gown, and her face was white. She said they would have to spend the day with John. They were seven and nine years old. It was just after their parents had come back after being away for eighteen months buying timber. For eighteen months they had been living in the house with their aunt, John, and the other servants.

No one explained why they didn't get to go to the funeral. No one even told them their father had died, but they did not have to ask, because her sister had seen him lying there unmoving, and she had seen him through Marion in her mind.

In their button-up shoes, and holding John's hands, they clambered around the rock garden while the funeral took place. The sun was shining as they climbed into their jacarandas and pulled the little box they had installed there with a pulley, back and forth, writing one another long letters furiously, as though they couldn't hear one another, and drawing Mr. Big Foot.

XX

JOHN STANDS BEFORE *KSKATIE* ON THE LAWN, holding the letter in his shaking hands and looking at her, reading her book in the yellow deck chair. He remembers how he would tease her as a child. *Kskatie, Kskatie, Kskatie,* he would chant.

"Don't call me that, John," she would tell him, crossly.

But he would laugh and go on, until she folded her arms and stamped her foot. "She needs some teasing, that one," he told her mother. "Too serious."

"*Ninge tshesa,*" Kate says now, referring to the hot late November day, John gathers, smiling lamely at the few words of Zulu she still seems to remember. How could she have forgotten so much? Sometimes when she tries to talk to him in Zulu the strange French words come out instead, and she shakes her head at herself and laughs.

John smiles back now and nods, though the day does not seem particularly hot to him. Kate shades her eyes from the glare, as she reads. He imagines her eyes through the glare of light as green.

He would take them as little girls outside and tell them the secret stories of his people that he had heard himself as a child.

He told them about hunters and warriors, slaves and masters; about *Lumakanda*, the Destroyer, who was born a slave and accidentally killed his own mother in a battle; about *Mitiyonka* who was murdered by his own wife and daughters; about *Malandela's* brother, the Braggart, and many others.

The stories were the secrets of his tribe, but he told them because the little girls had learned to speak his language and were his white children, and because his own black children, who should have been listening to these stories, had been taken from him. He told them what he knew, because they had lost their own father when they were so young, and there was no one else to take his place. But he warned the little girls never to tell anyone else or write the stories down. When they grew older they might tell them to their children, but to no one else.

He remembers how the children made him laugh. They liked him to dress them up with flowers and the shells they brought back from the seashore in Natal, which he made into bracelets and bands for their ankles and foreheads. "I need a crown, John," they said, when they acted out the characters from his stories. They preferred the queens and the princesses, and sometimes he drew pictures to show them the way such women wore their hair.

John is now watching the children who are wandering around in the garden, as Kate and Marion used to do, playing in the flowers. They look almost as if they are dancing. Probably some damage is being done.

He closes his eyes for a moment, for he feels exhausted. His old bones ache, and there is a heavy weight on his chest from the fear of what is up ahead for them all. He would like to escape this trouble.

He sighs and clears his throat, for *Kskatie* is falling asleep in the sun, and he needs her.

"What is it, John? You have received a letter and you would like me to read it for you, is that it?" she says, as he stands there in the hot sun, his starched khaki uniform rustling slightly as he moves, not knowing how to voice his request.

As a child he remembers how she would sometimes read his letters. But he shakes his head. He has never really learned much English. He has been too busy polishing, and now her Zulu has almost gone. Not that they need many words to converse. He has only to look in her eyes, and blind as he is, he can see her distress, which is more than sadness. He does not wish to worry her further, but he has something serious on his mind that he must share with her, and so he hands her the letter and lets her read for herself.

"A letter to Dr. Marais?" she says, looking up at him. She asks why he wants her to read a letter addressed to her dead sister's husband? Why should she read it? What does he know about such a letter?

"I am sorry to have to inform you…" she begins to read aloud, and then falls silent.

"What do you want me to do about this?" Kate asks, her voice trembling with anger, when she has read the letter to the end. "What can I do about it now?" she shouts at him.

He explains, "Miss Marion wanted *Baas* Louis to go and see and explain about the mistake. She was crying when I brought tea, and she was reading the letter. Afterwards, she told him to go and see and explain."

"Explain?" Kate says.

"An *indaba*." This is what is needed surely, some sort of meeting and council.

"Marion wanted him to explain what had happened?"

John nods again. "There was a mistake."

"When did this happen?

"On the day," he says.

"The day she died?" Kate asks, and John nods his head again.

She rises, looks around the garden for the children, and calls them to her. Their grandmother and grandaunt are sleeping, and the children are to be good while she is away, she tells them. They are to go on playing whatever it was they were playing, and John is to watch over them. They are not to go near the swimming pool.

She will go now and get this over with, go and see this woman and find out what really happened. She looks at the address on the letter and notices it is not far; she will walk, for it will give her time to think of what to say. Like her mother, she talks to him as though she were talking to herself.

She seems to look him in the eye, and he imagines that she is shaking her head at him. She thanks him for bringing her the letter, though he understands she wishes he had never known about it, that she doesn't want to do what he is suggesting. He is certain she feels he is an old black man meddling in affairs that are not his, and like the *baas* she thinks it is pointless, that nothing will be accomplished except more sorrow. Does she not remember his telling her that the Zulus believe that their lives are a necessary connection between their ancestors and their children? Does she not understand that he is trying to warn her of what might be up ahead, that he wants her to know the truth, that in the end only the truth can save her?

He sniffs the air and looks up at the sky, gesturing at the gathering clouds to tell her he feels rain is coming. The ants are running in the kitchen as always at such moments, and he can smell it in the air and feel it in his old, aching bones. It is better she takes an umbrella and has Wilson drive her there in the car. "Storm coming," he warns.

XXI

I T IS AN EARLY SUMMER STORM. The sky is black. The rain turns to hail. It slashes at the awning, brutally. The hail makes Louis restless. He is bored, bored, bored.

The nurse leans closer to his bed. She looks at him curiously. "Just a summer storm," she says softly. He remembers the first time he went to Crossways. It was raining then, too, but not the kind of rain that turns to hail. He wants to go back there, to his children, to his rightful place. Surely there is no reason for him not to visit his children, to hold them in his arms.

He has called the house a couple of times over the last few days and then put down the receiver immediately. When the sister answered the phone, the sound of her saying, "Hallo! Hallo! Who is this?" exactly the way his wife did, made him feel what he hasn't felt for years: joy, exaltation. He remembered his old adoration. Where did it go? Could it come back with this other one? And beyond that: would she let him press her up against a tree, carry her off as he had done her sister? This one has tried to break away. But has she?

When the nurse came into the room he had smiled at her. She had smiled back. He wanted to tell her he was happy. He wanted to say Kate's name out loud.

"My birthday, next Sunday," he reminds the nurse.

XXII

THE WOMAN ANSWERS THE DOOR HERSELF, an unusual event in this part of town. Wilson stands before the door, holding the umbrella over Kate's head, the rain falling hard, beating on the black material. She grips the letter John has brought her. The woman is short and stocky, with blond hair, somewhat in disarray, held back with a snood from her square face. She wears a black dress, a single string of pearls, but, incongruously, no shoes on her stockinged feet. Kate can see into the hallway and beyond, into a large, formal lounge, a bowl of gladioli on the console in a glass vase. She smells roasting meat. Dinner must already be cooking. She must make this brief. She already regrets coming.

A little boy comes running up to the woman's side in short gray pants and a pink shirt. She recognizes his uniform, the same as Mark's. He is about the same age as Mark and must be in standard one. He holds on tightly to his mother's hand. Kate stares at him and then looks up at the woman, whose face turns gray. She gives a little, low gasp and puts her hand to her mouth. For a moment Kate, thinking she might fall, grasps her elbow to steady her, but she draws back immediately, collects herself, and apologizes. She says Kate looks so much like her sister, it gave her quite a turn. They had been at Wits together and studied languages, before the woman had gone into the law. Their children were friends. She read about the accident in the paper and offers her condolences.

"I'll only be a moment," Kate says to the woman and to Wilson, who goes back to wait in the car.

The woman motions for her to sit by her side on a burnt-orange leather sofa. She bends forward to pick up a tinker toy from the carpet. There are several, scattered around the room, which, despite its opulence, gives an impression of disorder. The woman hands the toy to her son and tells him to go play in his room for a moment, so that she can talk to the nice lady. The boy holds onto his toy and his mother's hand and scowls darkly. Kate looks down at his pale face, the dark hair falling over the forehead, the rings under the large eyes. Under any other circumstances she would have told the mother what a handsome boy she had.

Instead, she says, "We thought I should come and see you," not mentioning, of course, who her conspirator is. What was John thinking? "My sister wanted her husband to come and speak to you." She looks up at the woman, who says nothing. She's not going to make it any easier. Why should she?

Outside, the sudden rain has stopped, and the water drips from the gutters. She thinks she smells smoke, afraid the roast in the oven will burn. There is a long sad silence in the room. All she hears is the little boy in the room next door, dropping something on the floor.

She looks at the gladioli. She has never liked them, too stiff, too artificial, she thinks. She says, hesitantly, "There was, perhaps, the possibility of some mistake in this matter, as my sister seems to have believed?"

The woman's dark eyes flash at her with rage. She seems to say with her eyes, "Are you completely insane!" She says bitterly, raising her voice a little, "There was no mistake, I assure you. Though, under the circumstances, you should know, we are no longer pressing charges. I gather your brother-in-law has been severely affected, brain-damaged, by the accident?"

She looks at the woman and then nods her head, but she wonders now just how damaged he is, how convenient is his stay in the hospital. Is he simply hiding out, biding his time? What is he planning?

She sees her sister again as she was the last time they met in Geneva, walking around the old city together, sitting out in a public square, drinking wine, talking with that old feeling of being at ease with someone who could understand every nuance. She remembers her sister talking about money, of all things. She had said, "What would we do if we had no money at all? How would we manage?" Certainly Kate's translations do not keep her alive, or even her teaching. Only the money their father left them has enabled her to live without worry.

There was no need to finish her sentences. Sometimes she felt herself moving her lips as her sister spoke, as though she were speaking her words for her. Yet how little she had understood. Or had she understood and not cared enough to act?

She remembers the accountant walking over the bridge sporting the new briefcase her sister had given him. She stood in the street to say good-bye to her sister, watching the short cream sleeves of the dress they had bought together, beating against her plump, honey-colored arms like wings. She put her arms around her sister to say good-bye. How could she have let her go?

What should she tell her mother about this matter?

The woman offers her a cup of tea, but she shakes her head, saying it is late. There are things she wants to know but dares not ask.

She ventures, "Your son is back at school now. He is…"

The woman looks at her. She says curtly, "My son's life will never be the same." Kate nods and impulsively reaches out to grasp the woman's hand, but the woman withdraws hers, as though Kate might contaminate her, infect her with her brother-in-law's crime.

As Wilson drives her slowly back to the house through the wet streets, and dripping trees, they talk. She sits beside him in the front of the car, reminds him of what he once said to her, and asks him how he is, and what is happening in this country now for the black people.

"There is terrible poverty, and more and more people disappear. They round up people on the slightest pretext, throw them into prison because they don't have a pass, or because the one they have is not in order. All our leaders are in prison. The police use torture and kill anyone who gives them trouble. Everyday there are hangings, beatings, frightful things. We are frightened all the time. But we are still full of hope," he says.

She looks out the window at the setting sun. She finds herself saying to him, "It's a dreadful place for all of us. Unspeakable things happen here. I want to get away as soon as possible," but she knows that she will not be able to do so. She will have to return the accountant's calls. She will have to find out what he wants to tell her. Perhaps she will have to see a lawyer. She will have to confront Louis.

The trouble is, she is not used to dealing with white men. In a way they have always seemed strangers to her, dressed up in suits. She is used to John in his khaki shorts, and to her boarding-school teachers in skirts. Rene, in his bow tie, is the exception, but he is a foreigner. And he is an impatient man. How much of this could he understand?

XXIII

A FTER THEIR FATHER DIED, John was the only man in the house. It was he who took care of them now. He taught them how to ride their bicycles, flapping the dishcloth at them and shouting "*khale, khale,*" as they wobbled down the bank. He walked them to the school bus, walking a few feet behind them, head held high, carrying their satchels, as though they were *assegais,* and he were protecting them from marauders. He took the cigarette from her mother's fingers, stubbed it out in the ashtray, and carried her over his shoulder carefully up the stairs. He lay her down on her side ever so gently on her wide bed, closed the shutters, removed her high-heeled shoes from her small feet, loosened her belt, and carefully unbuttoned the tiny, cloth-covered buttons of her chiffon dress.

They knew him by the rustle of his starched khaki uniform, his tapping of the bottle-opener against the cool drinks to ask them which one they wanted at lunch time, the rasp and swish of his polishing; he polished the silver with a toothbrush, the shoes, the soles of the shoes. They knew him by his chuckle and by the sound of his voice, when he told his stories of things they could not see, of all the invisible, lurking dangers.

Other men they knew from books: Heathcliffe, Mr. Rochester, 'umble Uriah Heep, with the limp, damp hands, Henry the Eighth, who chopped off Anne Boleyn's head, Peter the Great, who used a serf to demonstrate a torture machine, Louis Quatorze, who fell into a fish pond as a boy like a fool, and the men from the houses of Lancaster and York, who fought one another during the Wars of the Roses until they were joined by marriage. They drew the red and the white roses overlapping in their exercise books.

When their mother moved Uncle Charles into the small blue bedroom next to theirs, he discovered and read their fictive diary, taking the stories they made up for fact, and revealing them to their mother. He looked through all their things when they were away at school. He burst in to sing them funny songs while they were in the bath in the evenings, locking the door behind him.

He sang, "Susanna's a funny woman," clapped his hands, bent a leg up behind him, and danced about, turning red in the face. They laughed. He offered to wash them, but they said they were too big. They wouldn't do it properly, he knew they wouldn't. He took up the flannel, knelt down on the mat by the bath, and soaped it up.

Then he said, "Come, now, *Mademoiselles, pliez! pliez!*" as though they were in ballet class. He made them bend their knees and open up their legs, so that he could wash them down there, until they were nice and clean. Then he let them lie back in the warm water. He lifted up his hands and made spidery movements with his thick fingers in the air. He said he was going to have to tickle them all over, and he shook his shoulders and head with pleasure, so that his dark hair flopped over his damp forehead like a dog's.

They told him they didn't like to be tickled, please not to tickle them, and they kicked up the water in the air, but he said he wanted to tickle them so badly, he just had to, he must, he must. It was all their fault, because they were so terribly, deliciously tickleable, and what could he do?

They turned red and pressed their spines to the back of the bath. They kicked their legs at him, wetting his shirt. He took it off, and they saw his plump tummy and the curly dark hairs on his chest. He threw his shirt on the floor and sweated as he tickled their necks, their under-arms, and their tummies. He said he was going to tickle them where the soft hair would soon grow, like a pussy cat's.

They screamed that it would not, that they had no hair there and never would. He whispered in their ears, "I'm going to tickle your little pussies. Little pussies like to be tickled," and he laughed and tried to tickle them between their legs. He tried to slip his fingers between their lips down there and flutter their *gnomies*.

They were being silly girls, they must not make so much noise, he said, or their mother would hear and spoil their fun. He said they must lie still. He pressed himself against the side of the bath and groaned.

John heard them from the kitchen, where he was cooking dinner. He ran up the stairs to the bathroom and beat on the door. He shouted to let him in, that he needed to get in to clean up, that the water was dripping down into the kitchen below.

Uncle Charles wiped his face and chest with the wet flannel. He put his shirt back on and tucked it into his trousers, telling them to calm down now. They were getting overly excited and would have to go to bed without any supper if they were not good and quiet. Very quiet. Then he unlocked the door and told John to clean up the floor, because the girls had made such a terrible mess, just look at the terrible mess they had made. He slipped out of the bathroom and went downstairs to their mother and Dottie and the tray with the drinks.

John looked very cross and solemn. He said, "Just look at this mess. What happened?" They explained about the tickling in Zulu, and he sighed and shook his head.

Afterwards, when they were in their pajamas and dressing gowns and had eaten their supper in silence at the wooden table in the kitchen, their mother told them to come and say good night and give Uncle Charles and Aunt Dottie a kiss. She said they looked so nice and clean and thanked Uncle Charles for bathing them, and had they thanked him for taking such good care of them?

XXIV

THEIR MOTHER COULD NOT BEAR TO DROP THEM OFF HERSELF, SO she had Wilson drive them there. She stood in the doorway and watched them go off down the long driveway. John opened the white gate and waved. They watched him disappear through the back window of the car, as they drove under the jacaranda trees.

Kate was eight and Marion ten when they first went. They asked their mother to send them away, because they wanted to get away from the relatives in the house and also because all the popular girls were boarders and the day girls were left out.

Marion resided in the Middle School, a graceful nineteenth-century Dutch gabled building which lay at the end of a long alley of ancient oaks. Kate, in the Lower, was in the dull, long modern, red-brick building on the side of the gray-green hill. In the day she slipped slowly and silently down the long school corridors, hugging the walls or played a desultory game of sevens in the dry garden. At night she lay weeping in her bed in the long dormitory.

She felt, without her sister, her mother, or John, without the language she had always spoken with him and her sister, as though part of her were missing, a limb or a voice. She had left some essential part of herself behind in the garden at Crossways. She had lost the ability to speak for herself. She seemed now to inhabit a twilight zone between the English and Zulu worlds. She belonged to the world of the Zulu language with its different words, its different concepts of time and space, its complicated declensions, the world of the garden, of the characters and animals from John's stories, a world of the imagination, of freedom to invent and to be whatever she wished to be; and she found herself lying there alone in a dormitory in a long, neat row of beds beside the sleeping girls, an English-speaking child, learning English poetry with the spring in April and the summer in June. These were two opposing parts. She was *Kskatie* in her own mind and she was supposed to be this Kate to others. But her lost world was always with her, a voice in her thoughts.

It was at that moment that she became fascinated by the act of translation. On her first day in class she stood up and in a moment of distraction, when her name was called, greeted the teacher in Zulu instead of English—*Sawubona, unjani?* she said which made the children titter. They called her a white kaffir. She came to think of translation as a conjuring act, almost magical, the total transformation of a text from one language into another.

For she continued to think in Zulu with the words she and her sister had learned from John, as though these were her true words, this world hers. Her older sister, who had come with her to boarding school, was her only link with her lost paradise.

She would wonder what her sister was doing now, standing lost on the dry school lawn, looking up at the blank, white sky. Would she go up to that girl over there, the one with the pigtails reading her comic book on the lawn, and try to talk to her? Or would she climb the loquat tree and hide her solitude in the dark branches, dreaming? What would she dream?

Her sister came on Saturday mornings, when she was allowed to climb the hill between the Middle and Lower school to help her wash her hair and clean her hairbrush, to sit with her on the lawn in the sun, drying her hair and playing records on the gramophone. She sat and waited for her sister on the lawn with her hair greasy from a week without washing because of the drought. Her sister emerged, finally, climbing carefully through the hedge with the white flowers like small diamonds, picking blackjacks from her socks. Her sister smiled at her absently and called her name, the one John had given her because of her initials on the christening cup he polished, *Kskatie*. She ran to her, but her sister wouldn't let her hug her anymore or talk to her in Zulu. Looking around self-consciously, "Don't be a silly baby," she said, "for goodness sake, speak English!"

Her sister seemed in that moment to be all the things she had ever wanted to be with her large, wide-spaced, dark eyes, her lush, dark eyelashes, her high, heart-shaped forehead, her gold skin, her blue-black curls, her tiny white-blue teeth. She knew, even then, even at eight, in some obscure, terrifying way that her sister's beauty would not and could not last. Her sister seemed impossibly graceful, too full of light, incandescent.

Her sister, at ten, was hopeful and plump and shining. She, on the other hand, at eight, already expected the worst. She was sallow-skinned, solemn, and awkward. Her sister seemed like fast-running water. Kate was sluggish, dragging herself down the corridors and into the dusty classrooms, hiding her head under her desk. She seeped like an underground stream, secretive and opaque. She was Moon to her sister's Sun. She belonged to the night. She shone only with her sister's reflected light. There were times when she wondered if she existed at all, or if she were just a voice in her head, recording, chronicling, translating the life of someone else into English.

XXV

WHEN HER SISTER TOLD HER that she was going to marry Louis Marais, the Afrikaans surgeon they had met at the party their mother had given for them, she followed her sister around with more than usual devotion. She picked up any clothes she might have forgotten on a chair in their bedroom and hung them up in the closet. She tidied her already tidy drawers, rearranged her pots and creams on the dressing table. She picked flowers from the garden and arranged them in a small glass vase on her desk. She helped her write her essays for her courses at the university from books she perused hastily at night in the bathroom, sitting on the floor, so as not to disturb her older sister, essays on subjects she half understood—Lévi Strauss's views on the South American myths, "The Raw and the Cooked." "Myths," she wrote, "according to Lévi-Strauss bring together two opposites, two divergent poles."

XXVI

HER SISTER LEFT THE HOUSE WITH LOUIS in the evening in the summer holidays. John had gone to his homeland to visit his wives and had not come back at the end of the month, when he was supposed to have arrived. From time to time when he went to his homeland he did not come back at the end of his leave. "No sense of time," Dottie would say, clucking her tongue. Kate worried that John might have fallen ill or had a mishap on the train, as he had once.

She was obliged to spend the long, dull hours on the veranda with Dottie, her mother, and Uncle Charles. She decided to leave the country as soon as she could. There was nothing more she could do for her sister. She would go to the French family their mother had found for them, a family of minor aristocrats in Paris. She would learn to speak a foreign language, French, the most subtle of languages.

She told people she was leaving for political reasons. It was, after all, 1960, the year of the massacre at Sharpeville. She said that if she stayed she would probably end up in jail, but, of course, that was not the whole truth.

She felt that with her sister established as a bride in the big house, she would find it quite unbearable to linger on out there. In France, she considered, she would be able to hide. Speaking another language, she would become a different person, as she had become at boarding school. She would be transformed.

Her sister objected, "But you don't even like French much. I was the one who was good at it. You were always better at Latin, which is more like Zulu." Truly, she had preferred Latin, with its sentence structure and its declensions, which seemed closer to Zulu than to English.

"Won't you stay for the wedding, at least?" her sister said, tears in her eyes, staring at her with her tranced, fixed stare. She put her arms around her, begging her to be her bridesmaid, to carry the train of the long white satin dress Madame Vlamos, the Greek dressmaker, was preparing. Her sister said, "And you must be the one to catch the bouquet!" but she pulled away and told her she just couldn't do it. She didn't know how to explain, but she felt she needed to escape, if she were to survive. It was a sort of obligation.

She refused to be her sister's bridesmaid. She would not follow her down the aisle or catch the bouquet. She would not be one of the chosen. She would remain on the periphery. Her work, she felt, would prevent her from making the kind of compromises marriage required. For so long she had been afraid of living alone, glad to be surrounded by people constantly. Now she would have to live on her own.

She told John she was leaving, when he at last arrived back, looking gray, thin, and tired. She said she felt she had to go to another country, that there was too much evil in this land. He told her that he understood how she felt, that she must do what she wanted to do, or felt obliged to do, but that he would miss her. He held both her hands in his own at the gate. He told her that this house would be empty without her, that his days would be long, and that he would not forget her. He lifted her suitcase into the car, stood at the white gate when she left, raising his hand in the air and calling out *"Hamba khale"* when she drove away.

PART TWO

I

"**N**O PROBLEM, I'll see to it," the concierge, Maria, says cheerfully in French over the telephone, no tiredness in her voice. A small, Portuguese woman given to tears, Kate can see her, gray hair pulled back from her face, wrinkled skin, misshapen shoes. Maria has sorted the mail daily, kept everyone's keys, swept the stairs, and raised a boy and a girl on her own in that tiny, dark space at the foot of the stairs. There is a shadowy husband, too, with a thick mustache, who comes and goes, doing something in construction, who also somehow fits into the small space.

Kate imagines her small apartment at the foot of the stairs, the dining-room table where the mail is sorted, the vegetables chopped, the homework done, the letters written. She recalls glimpsing the angle of the kitchen through the open door, where the soup bubbles endlessly. "Always put in a few carrots, adds sweetness, Mademoiselle," the concierge had advised her.

She promises to send on the mail, to take care of the cats, and to let the landlady know about the flat. She says she can surely sublet to a tourist or student, someone happy to take the furnished place in the Latin Quarter for a few months at a lowered rent. She could pack up the clothes left in the closets, put away the china, and few pieces of silver, and do a bit of cleaning. Not to worry, she'll make sure all is safe.

The concierge likes the idea of working for someone who is a celebrity, even if it is only indirectly. She is always propping up photos she finds of Kate against the mantelpiece, and whenever she entertains, a rare event, the concierge loves to come in and pass around the canapés and tell her friends about all the famous people who were there.

She envisions the chestnut trees outside her windows in Paris. It will already be growing cold and misty there. The leaves will be turning amber and falling to the ground. November in Paris. She loves the autumn there, the cool weather and the pale skies. She has never liked the heat.

She already wants a rest from the sun. The brief spring has fast changed into breathless summer. It is already growing hot in the afternoons. The flowers hang down heavy, and the jacaranda blossoms lie on the ground. She has taken the children into the pool and let them splash around. The older ones already know how to swim on their own, racing up and down the pool; only the little one wears water wings.

She thinks longingly of her cool rooms, shaded by the chestnut trees, which she has all to herself. She is used to spending hours on her own with her typewriter, her dictionaries, her books. She likes the myriad transformations of the same text, the permutations of the words, the varieties of La Fontaine's "La Cigale et la Fourmie," for example. She misses her walks under the chestnut trees through the lovely streets, the silences, the voices in her head, recording her movements like secret sharers of her existence.

She thinks of the small, cozy living room with the chaise longue covered with a crocheted rug, where she can lie and stare out the window at the Pantheon across the park or read the newspaper under the standing lamp or listen to her records. She thinks of the small bedroom, with her soft double bed, where her silver cats lay curled up waiting for her, and where she was lying in her lover's arms, when her mother called her in the night to tell her of her sister's death.

She has not yet told Rene about this decision to stay on in South Africa, though he has probably understood that she is not coming home just yet. He has been calling her less, and the last time she spoke to him on the telephone, he sounded angry and talked of going to his house in the south of France for the winter months to finish his latest book of poems. She has refused to translate these recent ones. She finds the work too laden with conflict, the syntax too broken, the message of negation too strident. But she cannot tell him this.

"I would lose too much in the translation," was her explanation.

"You cannot stay on out there indefinitely," he said that last time, "or you'll become like the rest of them. It's a terrible country." She could imagine him impatiently pushing his long, glossy hair back from his face.

"There are things that have to be settled before I can come back," she said, thinking of his hands like water on her body.

"Why you?"

"Because there's no one else."

By now the children allow her to put them to bed at night. They ask her politely to leave the light on for them. The oldest is the one who is the most fearful of the dark, though he pretends to be brave. The children call her name in the night for a drink of water or to close the cupboard door. "Kskatie," they, too, call her now.

Above all, she needs a whole night of uninterrupted sleep.

She realizes she has not been out of this walled garden for weeks, not since the visit to the mother of the little boy. She knows she will have to call the accountant to find out what he wanted to tell her, though what is still to happen is as yet unimaginable.

II

THE NURSE IS GETTING READY to leave him for the night. She glides around the room arranging things for him. They have moved him out of intensive care, but this nurse has come willingly along with him. He sits in his chair in his navy-blue silk dressing gown. It is the one with the small white boats that his wife gave him. He looks out the window. He has asked for the same nurse, who seems safer to him. Better the devil you know. Though she gets on his nerves. Besides, she is clearly besotted with him.

She sidles up closer to his chair. She smells of cheap perfume and Johnson's talcum powder and desire. She turns out the lamp. "Time to tuck in," she says and gives him a wink. He doesn't like women telling him what to do. He's had enough of that in his life. He would like to tell her to shut up, but he's careful with what he says. She might be useful.

Now the nurse looks down at him tenderly. He asks, "And what about the visit to the house? What about my children?"

She smiles and says, "Soon enough." They must have told her to talk to him like this. Are they trying to hold onto him? Have the police been in touch with them?

He wonders if he could just slip out of his bed tonight and run along the road to his house. He wants to stand in his garden and look up at the big bay window. He wants to imagine K.K. up there with them. He wants to get away.

The nurse puts her hand onto the back of his chair, brushes up against him. She lingers at his side. She would like to get into the bed with him, he can see. "You really want to leave us? Go back to your children?" the nurse asks, her voice trembling a little.

His children must be with K.K. now. She must be sitting in the nursery, reading them stories just as her sister used to, sitting in the old leather armchair in the pool of yellow light. He imagines the dark hair, the dark eyes, the slim wrists.

The nurse sighs and walks across the room, swinging her hips, going over to the foot of the bed. She stands there reading his chart. "A house in which suburb?" she wants to know.

He doesn't respond to that. She should mind her own business. She's probably angling for an invitation. Perhaps she would like to take his dead wife's place. She can tell well enough from the address that the house is not far from the clinic, just down the road.

He watches as the nurse looks around the room to make sure everything is in order. She adjusts the bedcovers, turning them back and pats the bed invitingly. He gets up and goes to the bed. She helps him settle in, solicitously.

She turns out the light. "Sweet dreams," she says longingly, not imagining that his dreams will be of Pottie.

III

"GOOD NEWS," John says to Julia Kempden when she comes into the kitchen after breakfast to tell him that *Kskatie* will be staying on with them to help with the children. It is early morning, and the kitchen smells of coffee and the eggs and bacon the young maid has been frying for the children. Though he does not eat pork, the strong smells of the morning are a consolation. He can also smell Mrs. Kempden's familiar perfume, and hear the chink of her gold bracelets, as she moves her arms about restlessly, while he sits polishing the silver and feeling the embossed patterns with his fingers. He sits before her, staring up at her as he rubs at each fork and knife, blindly, and the newspaper, placed beneath the silver to protect the table, rustles as he moves.

His *Nkosi* often comes into the kitchen at the start of her day, to give him her orders, she says, but really to talk to him while he polishes, for he knows she finds it soothing to watch him work.

"Will *Kskatie* want to move into the master bedroom?" he asks lifting his head.

"Good idea, John," she says. "She'd be more comfortable there, don't you think?"

He tells the young maid to go in there after breakfast and dust properly, air the bed, and put some fresh flowers on the dressing table. He tells her not to forget to sweep under the bed, and under the carpet.

A sense of satisfaction, of celebration, occurs in the kitchen. There is sunlight on the floor. The maid, who is down on her knees polishing the red tile, not hard enough, he is sure, though she is a strapping, young Xhosa woman with broad shoulders, stops and lifts her hands together to the ceiling in a gesture of joy and thanks.

"Kate may have her own reasons for staying on," her mother says to John sitting down beside him, and lingering on in the kitchen for reassurance.

She tells him of all the important things that happen in her life, and he gives her sage council, just as his ancestors did for their chiefs. She asks his opinion of the people she meets. He has advised her against marrying the many suitors who used to come to her to marry her for her money. There was an English lord she almost married long ago, who hung around the lounge smoking a pipe, but he put her off that one, too. "Common rubbish," he told her.

"But he's got a title, John, an *Induna*, and a country seat in England. He's in the House of Lords," she told him.

He shook his head. "But a *skelm*," he said.

"You are probably right, John, as usual," she said and laughed with admiration at his knowledge of the world. "I'm probably better off on my own," which in his opinion she certainly is.

So she, too, has remained alone, as he has, though he has taken other wives, which is customary for his people, though expensive, with the *labola* to be paid each time, and then the needs of a young wife, but his allegiance is to his *Nkosi*, and she appreciates it. She must be wondering what it will be like, having her daughter back in the house. He knows she can be difficult. *Kskatie's* problem is she runs away from things she does not want to face. But what would happen if she faced them?

Miss Marion's ghost has come again in the night to him and walked across his room in the long silk nightgown which trails behind and looks dusty to him, as though the ghost has been walking a long way. It never speaks to him, though he hears it suck on its teeth, always Marion's sign that she was anxious. It is not necessary for it to say anything. It just stops at the bottom of his bed, and stares straight at him, its eyes filled with reproach. John is still waiting for *Kskatie* to do what needs to be done.

"I know she wants to continue with her work, her translating," Mrs. Kempden says, and he can hear her moving about, picking up the spoons, and putting them down, "and she's got a boyfriend, after all. I think he's alright, though he's a poet, of all things. Writes incomprehensible poetry. Jewish, I believe, but that's alright. I'd rather she married a Jew than a Catholic, quite frankly. Why doesn't she just go back home, hey? You don't think she wants to stir things up, things best left alone, do you, John?"

It is enough to nod and sigh or smile. He understands everything, and often he has helped her with his good advice. He knows the way the world works, and what is in the hearts of men, and he warns her of the dangers around her, though he realizes that of the most dangerous matters he may not speak.

He thinks of his ancestors who invented a new kind of warfare, and how they came down through Africa, conquering all the other tribes, using the short stabbing spears and the horn formation to surround their enemies.

"Give me a cup of tea, will you," Kate's mother asks the young maid, who is now washing up in the kitchen sink. John can hear her wasting water, letting it run unnecessarily. None of them think of things like that. None of them remember to turn off taps or switch off lights. He remembers the old *baas*, Hans Kempden, who would go around switching off lights and turning off the taps in the garden. "You are the only one I can count on, John," he would say to him. "You know the value of things." John believes his ghost, too, must be watching over them all, keeping an eye on the wasting of his riches.

For these young ones, they are wrecking the earth and polluting the sky and killing the animals, the *skelms*. What will happen to the children of these children? He says something sharp to the maid in Xhosa which he speaks, and she snaps back at him. No respect for his age and lineage. Does she not know who his ancestors are, the battles they fought with great bravery?

John just sighs and shakes his head, but he feels Mrs. Kempden has a point here, and he, too, is concerned about what may happen.

IV

IT IS DAWN. She lies in the whispering silence and the heavy heat of the blue room, unable to sleep. She is used to her small, dark bedroom in Paris on the second floor, where she can hear the rumble of cars, voices and sometimes, in the summer, when the windows are left open, a radio blaring. Here the first light penetrates the curtains, and all she can hear is the birdsong of early morning, the wind in the leaves. She shifts and turns restlessly between the sheets, missing being curled up into Rene's long, thin body.

She misses talking to him. He is a stern man or appears to be. The child of holocaust victims who had left Germany for France when he was a small child, only to be sent from Paris to the camp in Beaune-la-Rolande and then deported to Auschwitz, he had narrowly missed being gassed himself. He spent the war in the countryside near Paris in Chantilly with a wealthy Christian family who owned horses and felt obliged to shelter him, but never treated him as they did their own children. He is more at ease with small children, eccentrics, and old ladies, with whom he is invariably patient, kind, and courteous. He does not always feel it is necessary to be courteous with other people. "You are too polite," he says to Kate. "Rude people are much more likely to be taken seriously." He says he does not believe in charm, a cheap trick and substitute for real service or interest. Yet she has seen him taken in by it like everyone else.

He does not attempt to charm in his work, she knows. He has become increasingly difficult to read. He coins new words, especially compound ones, and he divides words into syllables, a trick she finds tiresome. He carries the process of condensation and dislocation to an extreme in his cryptic, spare poetry. And though he maintains he is not religious, she feels his poems have become increasingly God-forsaken. They make her sad. He was briefly a medical student in Tours, and in his work, he often writes about the suffering body.

Kate remembers suggesting Rene do some publicity for his first book, which was published by a good house, the one she translated with such difficulty and success.

"Publicity?" he said and looked at her blankly.

"You know, readings, panels, radio interviews, things like that. So that people know about the book."

"We don't do that here," he said sententiously, and not entirely truthfully, after all.

But his American publisher was happy to arrange what she called a "tour-ette" for her translation. She went to New York, Boston, San Francisco, Portland, and Seattle. She read and even tried bravely to answer questions about the work. At first, standing up and facing an audience, she could hardly breathe. She was afraid she would fall to the floor in a faint, as she had done as a girl. She couldn't think of what she would say, but she surprised herself. She found she was quite good at answering questions. She would hear herself speaking, saying things that sounded intelligent, the words just springing forth, as if from some secret source.

When she was asked about the meanings of Rene's poems, she talked a lot about the "process." She said that it was not so much what was said, but what was withheld, that was important. She spoke of the meaning that lay in the silences, the gaps between the words. She spoke of the progression of the imagery rather than the argument. She commented on the dialectic of dark and light that ran through the work. She managed something about the unconscious being structured like a language, as Lacan had pointed out. She told her audiences Rene's words were not to be considered as windows to meaning or even to the factual world, but rather that they were themselves narrative objects with arbitrary referents, just words with palpable shapes and audible sounds, forming rhythms with their lines.

All of which impressed people considerably, she realized, seeing them staring up at her, though Kate was not quite sure what it all meant. She had the feeling someone else was speaking through her.

She remembers the visit a former girlfriend of Louis' made to them years ago, before he married her sister. She had tried to tell them something, really. She must have found their telephone number in the book and taken the trouble to call them up. She said she would like to come and talk to them. Perhaps that was her mistake. Strillie, her name was.

They said they would be delighted to meet her, that she must come to morning tea, because they thought morning tea would be quick. They gave her directions.

She remembers it clearly now, as she lies in the bed in the blue room, hoping the children will not wake, not quite yet, that she can lie here for a few moments more in the heat and the silence with the door yawning open between her room and theirs and the early morning sunlight honeying the floor.

She remembers looking out the window and seeing the little, white Volkswagen convertible coming up the driveway under the alley of jacarandas.

It was a winter morning in June or July, the grass dry, leaves on the ground, bare branches like scarecrows against a white sky. The air was smoky with winter fires. John opened the door to let the girl inside and ushered her into the shadows of the sunken lounge with the curtains drawn on the bright morning sun and the grand piano open in the corner.

They were all there, all four of them, she is sure of that: their mother and Dottie, she and her sister. Strillie, a big, dark-haired girl with a little hair on her upper lip, seemed confused, staring at them. She was not sure who was who, until they explained it was Kate's sister who was marrying him. Even then she had difficulty distinguishing them and kept calling them by the wrong names. Dottie served the tea, fussed with the scones with her trembling hands, and kept dropping the teaspoons, giggling nervously.

They tried to be polite, of course, sitting there side-by-side on the sofa, in their identical single strings of pearls and mohair twin sets, pale blue jackets and navy pleated skirts and flat English brogues, with the tongues, sitting straight-legged, feet slightly to the side, the way they had learned to sit in deportment class.

Her sister explained that she was studying anthropology at Wits, and she said she had just finished her matric at Rhodean. Her sister would start a sentence, and then Kate would finish it, and they would laugh, putting their hands to their mouths.

They gave her tea, Marie biscuits, and fresh scones with cream and even offered her sherry, though it was only eleven in the morning. They invited her to take a walk around the garden, to stay for lunch, which she declined. They kept waiting for her to say something.

At first she seemed a little distracted by the food, the silver tea service, all the silver spoons, perhaps by Dottie's trembling hands. She tucked into the scones with the raspberry jam and clotted cream. Perhaps she hadn't had any breakfast. She just sat there in the big, shadowy lounge on the silk sofa, eating and procrastinating for a bit, obviously not quite sure how to put it to them.

Perhaps she found them difficult to talk to, they thought afterwards. They were aware that they gave off an air of stiffness and reserve. They were really only used to talking to one another or to John. There was the dip at the corners of their lips, the distant gaze, the slightly sloping shoulders, despite the reaching for the ceiling with the tip of the head, they had been taught in deportment class, as though thrusting out the chest and showing off their breasts might have insulted her. The deportment woman had said nothing about breasts, which might have been more to the point. Really, they were just waiting for her to leave, to go back to their own conversation. She didn't know them. She just kept on eating those scones.

Finally, her sister put down her teacup and asked if there might be something the girl wanted to tell them.

She just blurted it out then. She said she had seen the announcement in the paper, and she begged her not to marry him. Both sisters just sat there politely, sipping their tea, smiling, nodding their heads. Their mother said it was too late, that the invitations had already been sent out, and all the wedding plans made. She admitted she, herself, had been somewhat against the match, initially, him being an Afrikaner, a Boer, after all, but she had reconciled herself to it.

She said, "Do come and see the presents." So what could the poor girl say? Probably she was curious, too. They all rose and trooped up the stairs to the study to show her the splendid wedding presents, spread out on a starched damask cloth, covering the trestle table, silver bowls and open chests of silver cutlery, Venetian glass vases in beautiful blues and reds, a small nest of Hepplewhite tables, with delicate marquetry, a family heirloom sent from their maiden aunts in Kimberley.

Their mother insisted Strillie come and see the car she had given the couple as a wedding present. There was something rather childlike about her showing off all the gifts, like a girl showing her toys. In a way, you could say it was showing off, but she seemed to take such real pleasure from all the lovely things, you could hardly hold it against her, and it must have been difficult to refuse to see the presents. Besides, she was probably fascinated, the way one is by the lives of the rich, for no good reason at all. So they walked through the house, across the lawn, and down the steps, into the dimly lit garage. Strillie admired the silver car shining there. Someone had polished it, and it shimmered even in the dim light of the garage like a ghost.

When they were back inside the lounge again, their mother went off to fetch Uncle Charles as well, and he shuffled in, in his wide-legged trousers and flat feet. He said something banal about time curing all ills. Their mother told Strillie very proudly that Uncle Charles was giving her daughter away, that the wedding was to be held at St. Martin's-in-the-Field, the stone church in Parktown, and that her daughter would wear a white satin dress and carry a lily-of-the-valley bouquet. She even told her the name of the dressmaker and that she would be most welcome if she should like to come to the ceremony.

The girl tried to insist, though obviously she was not convincing. She said, "Don't do it. I beg of you not to."

Their mother twisted her single string of pearls and said brightly, "I'm sure you, too, will receive a proposal soon, my dear."

Dottie said, "Such pretty hair," and smiled at her ingratiatingly and touched her hair, as though she were a doll.

There was a moment of silence, while they all looked at Strillie and then down at the carpet.

Then Kate said, "Why are you saying this to my sister?"

That was the moment when she should have explained it.

She looked around the room with all the pale Pierneefs on the walls and then down at her feet. But all she could manage was to ask them to trust her, could they not all trust her? She knew what she knew. They might have seemed innocent, and they were in a way, but they were also suspicious, the way rich people often are. They did not really trust anyone. They were always wondering if someone was going to ask them for a favor of some kind. At that moment they were trying to calculate her motivation, rather than just listen to what she had to say.

V

HE SAT ON THE SOFA next to Pottie and unbuttoned his checked shirt. "What are you doing to me, Lou?" Pottie asked, his voice trembling. He slipped his hand over the red fur on the stomach and downwards. Pottie said, "For God's sake!" He found the old man's cock. He rubbed it slowly, up and down. He made him so hard, the old man moaned. "No one but you has touched that for a while," he said and laughed at the flushed face, at the open mouth with a little spittle in the corner.

Poor Pottie had never married. He had lived alone all those years in his small, untidy house with his plants and his books of Latin and Greek, and the battered, stand-up piano where he had taught Louis to play "Claire de Lune." Louis would bet Pottie had never had a lover, though he must have dreamed of one for years, as he lay between his sheets. To have this happen at fifty. Poor Pottie called on his God. Louis had to put it in his mouth, there on the old couch. He bent down and sucked him off. It was his way of saying thank you for the scholarship. That was all.

But after that, of course, Pottie wanted more. They always did. He wasn't willing to let it go at that. He talked about love. *God!* As though love had anything to do with sex. Pottie didn't understand it was simply a service. That it meant nothing to him. Then Pottie lost it completely. He kept calling him up. He begged for it. Wouldn't leave him alone. *Asseblief, asseblief, asseblief!* He was obliged to do something about it. Couldn't have the old man hanging around the house like that.

In response they fired him from the teaching job he had loved. From the boys. Soon after, someone found him hanging in his closet.

VI

THE SISTERS STROLLED FROM THE HOTEL at the top of the Spanish Steps toward the Bernini fountain below, making their way in the spring sunlight, through the throngs of people: vendors selling absurd, squeaking toys, postcards, pens; tourists milling aimlessly up and down or stretched out with abandon in the sun. The pink and white azaleas spread like bright scarves across the stone. It was late afternoon, the light softly radiant, the shadows long, the air still sultry. The boat-shaped fountain at the bottom of the steps sprayed with a cooling sound.

Her sister was talking about her husband. Louis was in such demand as a heart surgeon, she said proudly.

"I'm sure he is," she said, as a young man in tight, faded bluejeans came up the steps and asked her sister if she would have a light for his cigarette. While she hunted for matches, he asked her if he hadn't seen her somewhere before. She smiled a little uncertainly and shook her head. "*Sono sicuro di si,*" he said and grinned widely.

"I don't think so. People are always asking me that," she said.

"Perhaps I know a relative of yours—*una sorella*? *una cugina*?" he insisted. Her sister laughed at the man, but she pursed her lips and told him to leave them alone.

Her sister blinked at her and said, "People are always asking me for directions, which, of course, I never know. They always think they know me—I must have that sort of face," and went on talking about her husband. He operated often, his nurses adored him, his secretary adored him, his patients adored him, his friends, especially Serge. She added, "He says he adores me, worships the ground beneath my feet."

"And so he should," she said and glanced at the downward cast of her sister's eyes, the slight flush of blood on the cheekbones.

"Of course, sometimes the patients die, often in fact. Heart and chest operations are very difficult, after all," her sister explained with that remote expression in her eyes.

"I'm sure they are," she said, looking at her face, the big, blinking eyes. But when the patients survived, they were ever so grateful, Marion explained. He was particularly good with post-operative care, attentive and skilled. He believed in making his recovering patients comfortable.

"That's what mother always says," Kate remarked, noticing suddenly her sister's dark eyes glistened with tears. "Something wrong?" she asked, brushing off another vendor who was flashing a long chain of postcards at her. Her sister shook her head, demurring, but she continued to weep. They sat down on the edge of the fountain, listening to the spray of the water falling, just as it did at Crossways.

He was hardly ever home, working such long hours, and her sister missed her, she said, putting her hand on her arm. The house seemed so empty. Her sister, even after her three children and her sorrows, was still slender, though her face was paler, dusted over with powder, sitting with a blue scarf around her long neck, in a short-skirted dress. It was the time of very short skirts. She blinked back tears in the Roman sunshine. She wore her dark curls a little longer now, parted to one side, falling in soft waves on her cheek. Marion brushed her hair back from her face and lifted her hand in a wan gesture and said she had never found anyone else she could talk to the way she could talk to her.

"The language of childhood," Kate said.

Marriage could be a very lonely place, her sister added. It could shut you off from the rest of life and yet not replace what was lost.

She said, "Don't worry, darling, I have no intention of marrying. I prefer my loneliness," and put her arm around her sister's shaking shoulders and thought of the lonely streets of Paris, which she tramped with a voice in her head. She thought of Rene and how she had replied, when he had asked her to marry him, "What for?"

She had meant that she was quite happy as she was with him, but naturally he had been hurt and had rushed off, slamming the door. This was a moment when he had not found her too polite. But he had come back the next morning and told her he wanted to talk to her, as her sister was doing now.

When her husband came home at night, he seemed exhausted and often bad-tempered. He shouted at her, at the children, the servants, complaining of small things which had no importance. She had ended up hiring many servants—so many people needed work, after all—to help with the children, the big garden, the rambling house, the needs of her mother and aunt. "I don't think he really likes our house," she said.

Kate hunted for a handkerchief and gave it to her sister, telling her, as their mother used to tell them, that she must seize the day, before it was too late. If she was unhappy, if he neglected her, she must lead her own life. There was no need for her to take his criticism lying down, no need at all: she must defend herself.

Her sister glanced back, saying she didn't understand, that it was not as simple as that. Her chin trembled, and she wiped her eyes, as she said she suspected her husband was unfaithful to her.

"What do you mean, suspect?" she asked sharply and turned toward her sister, who only blinked her blue, tear-filled eyes, and shook her head.

She said scornfully, "You don't have to put up with something like that, for goodness sake! Why do you? I would never let a man treat me in that way! Take a lover. Why don't you take a lover?"

For the first time there were silences between them, things left unsaid, out of loyalty, shame, or fear. She does not know which. She thinks of all the silences of women, covering for their men, and for themselves.

VII

H E LIKED TO GET AWAY from Crossways on Sunday afternoons.
He liked to leave the vast, lonely house, and its light-
colored, hollow rooms, with their big, cut-glass bowls of
flowers. He liked to escape all those women: the mother-in-
law in all her glittering pearls and diamonds, the aunt, the
sister who came to visit as often as she could and his wife.
There were too many of them for him.

He hated the long, boring Sunday lunch parties with
everyone voicing clichés. He hated the decorous tennis parties,
everyone in white, calling out five-love, or even worse, the
swimming parties, with the women sitting under the
umbrellas in their two-piece suits, sipping lemonade and
tittering. They talked about their children, their servants, and
their boring books, while the men talked about business or
golf. They were all wealthy, sheltered people. They knew
nothing about real life. They had never known the pressure of
arduous, endless study, the humiliation of the outsider.

Sometimes he would be so bored, he would have to slip out
the French doors in the dining room and go into the garden.
He would go to the old colored gardener, who knew where to

find a *rook*. That might liven things up a bit. His wife would look into his eyes, catching him up with her "You have been smoking *dagga* again, haven't you?"

"Life around here is too bloody boring to take neat," he would respond. She would sigh. She would try to understand, always, but she couldn't, really. She was never bored. "You can always read a book," she would say with that air of wonderment on her face. She always seemed surprised by his life, his stories of the child dying on the operating table, of the old woman whose death he had had a hand in. She knew nothing about men, or anyway white men. She and that servant John were always jabbering away in Zulu. She never bothered to learn his language properly. She knew nothing about him, her husband.

Oh, she tried her best. She was always an obliging girl, his wife. She was thoughtful, polite, and kind. Always so calm, unflappable, and restrained. She was the most reserved person he ever met. Almost, at times, as though she were not quite with you. There was a vagueness about her that infuriated him, a lack of precision in her thoughts and acts. She dithered. She said one thing and then the opposite. Half the time, he couldn't understand what she had said.

And though she would deny it, there was always the difference of class and culture between them. She spoke with a different accent. She used different words to swear. She swore in French, *merde*, she would say. *God!* She used different words to talk about the private parts of her body. "Got to go for a wee," she said. It infuriated him, set his teeth on edge, like chalk scraping across a blackboard.

She was, above all, English. You couldn't get away from that. Her ancestors had murdered his in the camps. She had different historical references. They had not read the same books. They had not studied the same things. She knew nothing about science, about how the body worked.

Her orderliness made him uneasy. She wanted everything in its place. She wanted to rule him. He came to hate what had dazzled him: all the net curtains, the velvet pelmets, the silver sugar bowls, the flowers, the polished parquet floors he was not supposed to soil. "Think of the servants, Louis," she would say. "Take your boots off when you come in from the garden. You're dirtying the floor, darling." She called everyone darling.

And she was too close to the black servants in the house. He didn't think it was healthy. There was a confusion of roles. She spoiled them, was overfamiliar with them, overpaid them.

She had always had money. It had no meaning for her. She had no real understanding of what his life was like. She had no idea of what it was like to have to work as hard as he has. She had no idea of being careful even with small things like the soap. He remembers how she would laugh at him when he counted out the change, before he put down the bills, and would sometimes forget to put down the bills and have to be reminded. You could see the difference in the way she just stood there being who she was, a Kempden. It was never enough for him to just be who he was.

On Sundays he preferred to take his children swimming at the public pool on his own. He didn't mind paying the low entrance fee. He might even buy them ice-cream sandwiches and orange sodas. They would sit on the grass or on towels or in the stands in the sun by the water with all the other families. The children preferred it too, he was certain. Sometimes he took them to watch the tennis matches or the swimming heats.

He would often bring a picnic, chicken-in-a-basket, chips, colas. He'd tell John where they were going. He would get him to pack the basket and put it in the car for him. Then he could lie on the grass and watch his children swim. The older ones had both learned early. Even the baby would go in the water on her own with her water wings. He would watch them, just as he had watched their mother and her sister long ago. It made him remember how he had felt about them then. He remembered M.K. on the diving board, almost hitting her head.

He loved those ordinary Sunday moments. He loved the noise, the throng of people at the public pool, the sun. He would lie by the pool in his tight blue swimsuit on a towel on the grass with his children splashing joyfully in the water. The people around him, many of them Afrikaans-speakers, looked on admiringly. He liked being with his own kind, people whose language, whose customs he understood.

"What lovely children you have," they would say, not waiting to be introduced in their friendly, open, jovial way, as they walked past. Or "Hey man! What good swimmers you've got there!" Or they would say, "What a good father, hey, giving Ma a bit of a rest on Sunday, are we?" He would nod and smile with modesty. He would feel for a moment part of a community, a crowd. The emptiness, the boredom would seep away. Sometimes he would have the opportunity to talk to some young man or woman who caught his fancy. They might make plans for a further meeting, later that night. But even if that didn't happen, he was happy.

Sometimes he would take the children to visit Serge, who lived near the pool. Serge was good with *die kinders*. He would find a game to amuse them, and once in a while they could slip into the other room on their own and have a little fun.

VIII

ONE TIME AFTER SEVERAL YEARS OF MARRIAGE, her sister left her husband and children behind and came to Paris and stayed with her for a week. After lunch she would put her work away and walk with her sister through the lovely streets, their arms linked. They walked together, as they had done as girls, under the chestnut trees, which lined the street where she had found her small, shady flat. They spoke of many things. Walking beside her sister, she had the impression she had never been away from her, that they could pick up where they had left off.

Her sister told her a curious story about a friend and asked her advice. "This is what happened," she said in her deadpan voice. "What would you have done?" The friend, who by some strange coincidence was also married to a young Afrikaans doctor and lived in a large house in Johannesburg, had given a party at her house for her husband's birthday, inviting all his relatives. The relatives came up from their farms in the Great Karoo to stay in the big red brick house. There were many children that weekend, splashing in the pool, jumping on the trampoline, eating the food. The friend, who was as good a cook as she, had made heaps of food, roasted pork, gem squash, apple pies.

In the middle of the party on a summer evening, the roses in bloom, the sky wild with stars, all the food and drinks laid out on trestle tables under the trees, the friend was resting for a moment, eating a little dinner and sipping a glass of red wine, side-by-side with her in-laws, enjoying the party, when she realized her husband was nowhere to be seen.

She found him under one of the jacaranda trees, but he was not alone.

The friend's husband did such wonderful work, her sister told her with tears in her eyes. Who knows what happens to men who have to deal with life and death on a daily basis like that? One has to take that into consideration, don't you think? She told her that butchers at one time were given clemency if they had committed a crime, because of their profession. Her friend had been taught, as they had at school, to be compassionate, to forgive. Apparently, the friend's husband was so clever, always top of his class, passed his matric at sixteen, and so handsome; too handsome, perhaps. What should she have done?

Afterwards, when the friend had found her husband, he would say nothing to her about it. He wouldn't look her in the eye. He said it meant nothing, that he adored her, that she was the Queen of his Heart. They hardly spoke after that. What could they say?

The night had been sultry. Moths gathered around the moon-shaped lamp. The friend walked across the damp grass and looked toward the jacaranda tree. The husband was there with his back against it, pinioned, his head tilted as though he were staring up at the stars. The other young man, also a doctor, knelt before him, as though praying, though it was quite clear to the friend that the young doctor was not praying at all. Oh, no. She stood there in silence, all her dreams vanishing, falling through the air like the water over the wall into the pool. She watched in the moonlight while the water fell, and the moths went on gathering around the moon-shaped lamp, and her new family danced drunkenly to the big band, holding hands with her children on the lawn.

IX

H E REMEMBERS COMING HOME from the hospital early one afternoon. He just walked out of the operating room, unable to stay another minute. He told the house surgeon to take over and close up. He walked out without another word. He put down his instruments and stepped out from under the lamps. He went into the scrub room and removed his gloves and mask, throwing them into the basket, and stepped out into the light of day.

His wife had left the children behind with her mother and aunt. She had gone off to Rome to see her sister, or so she said. It was not long after she had found him in the garden with Serge under the jacaranda.

That afternoon, he found himself in a rage. He drove home much too fast in his Mercedes. He threw open the door. He entered the house and looked for the children. He saw the older ones sitting out under the jacarandas with old John, playing with their red and white blocks, piling them up in a tower. The baby must have been sleeping in her crib. Their grandmother and grandaunt knitted as usual in the deck chairs.

He kicked over the tower of blocks, swooped down and picked up both children out of the dirt. He carried them off, one under each arm, too stunned to scream. He threw them into the back of his car without a word, turned on the radio, and drove off with them.

He drove to the Vaal dam, where they keep a rondawel. A simple place, one room with a thatched roof, without any silver or fucking pelmets or parquet floors. He spent the night there. He remembers the clarity of the night. He went outside, leaving the children sleeping in their cots, for a long walk along the edge of the dam. He remembers the brightness of the stars, the thick, velvet darkness of the sky, the moon shining on the water. A dog barked in the distance. He rented a sailboat the next day. He took the children out on the lake behind the dam. They had all gone sailing together, while their mother was off fucking some goddamn Turk.

X

H E COULD HEAR THE *BAAS* shouting loudly for him. It was a summer evening, and he was taking a brief moment of reprieve before serving dinner. It was shortly after Miss Marion had come back from her trip overseas. She had told him she had been to Rome to see *Kskatie*, and they had talked, and her sister had given her good advice. From there she had gone on to Turkey. "Turkey was very beautiful," Miss Marion told him, standing in the dimly lit corridor that leads into the pantry, and he nodded his head, though he cannot imagine any place more beautiful than his own. "The sea, the beach, and old Roman ruins," she explained, "lovely, lovely. *Maningi muhle.*"

Now he was standing outside in the servant's courtyard, smoking his pipe in the cool of the dusk and thinking about his dead wife and children. He remembered the way they would greet him on his return to his homeland, how his wife would come running to him down the hill, his babies in her arms. He was remembering the feast she would prepare for him, the wild figs and honey cakes. He would sit before the fire and talk to her. He can still hear the sound of her voice, see her round smooth head blooming, the light falling around her like soft rain.

But at the urgent sound of the *baas's* voice, he had put down his pipe on the windowsill and left his memories and hurried inside. He climbed to the top of the carpeted stairs, two at a time, to see what the *baas* wanted of him.

At first, through the mist of his failing sight, he did not understand what had happened. He thought he might be seeing the first Mrs. Kempden's ghost on the stairs, as he had seen her before, trying to pull the scarf off her neck, moaning. Then he saw the three children crowding around the *baas* in their white viyella pajamas, flapping their arms like wings, looking like startled birds. The baby, who was still small then and could hardly walk, was hopping about on one foot and making a little moaning noise, and he was afraid she might fall down the steps, so he took her up in his arms. Lydia was calling her father's name urgently, and Mark just stood there staring, his cheeks flushed, lifting his arms up and down, as if he wished to fly off somewhere. They must have just come out of their baths, and he smelled their child smells of soap, water, and panic.

Then he understood why the *baas* was calling for them and what he wanted them all to do. "Come and watch me die," he was saying with drama, in Afrikaans, to his children, and to him, as if he were on some stage and not on the green carpet on the stairs which he had brushed by hand, down on his hands and knees very carefully with the brush and the dust pan just that morning, so that not one speck of dust remained.

He shook his head and clucked his tongue with consternation, as he saw the *baas* sprawled there at the top of the stairs, and the blood running down his wrists, which he must have cut with a knife, the blood running onto the green carpet and staining the spotless weave. He would have terrible trouble removing that blood, just as he had had once with the chocolate syrup, served with the ice cream, which had stuck to the cut-glass goblets after a dinner party. He had had to stay up past midnight trying to remove it without breaking the precious goblets.

He stood with the children, his hand on Mark's shoulder and Lydia clutching his leg, the baby now in his arms, and did as the *baas* asked him to do. He noticed that he was holding a letter in one of his hands, which he learned later had been in Miss Marion's handbag. He was able, afterwards, to hold the letter up to the light, and he recognized the color of the ink and the writing, and he knew how she was never any good at hiding things, and he presumed the *baas* had not liked what he had read.

He thought of how Miss Marion had called to him as a child, when she had accidentally stepped on her budgerigar, and how he had wrung its neck to put it out of its misery, and he had considered helping the *baas* in this task that he had begun, in a similar fashion. He was stooping over him and feeling his neck for the pulse, when Miss Marion had arrived and told him instead to help her carry her husband to the car, which he might have told her seemed like a mistake to him, if he had thought it was his position to tell her something of that sort.

So he had remained with the children and made them eat some dinner and told them a story, while she had driven the *baas* to the clinic, where he had recovered and then come back to make jokes about Turkish Delight.

XI

I T WAS NOT THAT HE WANTED TO CAUSE PAIN. Would he have chosen to be a doctor, a surgeon, if he had? Would he have wanted to stand on his feet an entire day or night to save a life, then? Why did he undergo all those years of training to learn how to do so, hey? What did she think the Hippocratic oath meant to him, anyway?

But it was the only way to stop her, to calm her down. For she did have a temper. You wouldn't have thought so, to look at her: she looked like a bloody angel. That was what was so deceptive. That was the problem. She looked like the calmest, quietest, sweetest woman in the world. And she was, most of the time. But when she got mad, all hell broke loose. She acted without thinking. Many women did. They kept talking about their bloody feelings! They refused to use the left side of their brains.

It was for her own good. It was for the good of their marriage. He was the one who held it together, goddamn it. He wouldn't let her get away. He couldn't let her go to anyone else. When she went off to Turkey to frolic with her lover, it was too much. It destroyed him. He had to make sure it didn't happen again. He made sure she was home for lunch every day. He had her followed to make sure she was behaving herself.

After a bloody good hiding, she'd be ready to show some sense. She would be ready for proper love. And so was he. A simple slap across the cheeks would do it, sometimes. Then she'd melt, and he'd get hard. He could slip his hand up between those plump thighs and spread those round cheeks. He could get his tongue into her cunt.

It was a pity it was necessary, but it was. He didn't care what the bloody psychologists had to say. It was like the Pope telling people not to use contraceptives. That bloke'd never had to cope with women, didn't know how hard they were to control, how they tried to take advantage, to take over your life, what it took to keep them in line, cut them down to size.

And she could be violent, herself. She could take any kind of insult, but only for a while. She would be patient beyond belief. But then she'd lose it. She would throw things. She even screwed off the top of the bedpost and flung it at him one day. She was bloody strong and bloody *stroppie* when she got mad.

Sometimes he couldn't handle her by himself, strong as he was. He'd have to call in one of the servants to hold her down. He'd call in one of the strong young women. That seemed more appropriate for bedroom work, which is what this was, after all. He'd get the young maid to come. He would tell her to hold her mistress down on the bed. There was a bit of pleasure in seeing the rich, white mistress held down by the poor, black maid—a nice reversal of roles, after all: a Kempden girl helpless on her back on the bed, the black maid pinning her with her strong, smooth arms. He liked to see the two women juxtaposed in this way. Black-on-white that became blue. He doesn't know much about paintings, but it looked like one to him. And it excited him, the coupling of two women. He would tell the maid to mount on the bed, too. "Get on top of her," he would say. She would lower her eyes and look at the floor. "Go on, what are you waiting for? Climb up. Isn't that what you want to do?" He would make her flip M.K. onto her stomach. "Hold her by the shoulders," he would command. She spread her legs across her mistress's waist. He liked to imagine the shame she must have felt. The maid loved it, he could see, in spite of herself—all that pent-up rage released. M.K. would try to lift her head. She would curl her lip and snarl. The maid would murmur to her to be calm. She would say to lie still, Madam, please.

Then he could take off his belt and lift M.K.'s skirt. He could give it to her hard across the bare bum. Sometimes he caught the maid's legs or even her back as well. He would have to keep at it for so long his arm would ache. It took her so bloody long to start to scream, but finally, she would beg for a reprieve. Even the maid would murmur that Madam had had enough, that the Master had hurt her. The maid would weep.

He believes it is a necessary though barbaric act. He has to admit there is pleasure in it. There is excitement. There's always violence in the sexual act. He is certain of that. But that's not why he does it: he does it for her own good.

XII

THE LOW WHITE HOUSE is very much like the others on the street. There is a small-fenced back garden and a dog somewhere, shut up in a kennel, barking sporadically. She catches a glimpse of washing fluttering on a line.

The front door is ajar and the accountant, Malachy, awaits her. A slight young man with reddish hair, he looks flustered, his pale, freckled skin, flushed. He greets her warmly, she feels, at the door. She also notices another man, who lurks about somewhere behind him in the small, low-ceilinged living room.

Malachy introduces her to him, but she does not catch the name. She wonders what he is doing here, and why he, too, has been invited on this hot afternoon. The lounge is furnished with a bar in the corner and some modern chrome chairs. She sits down on one of them, declines a cup of tea or a cigarette. She wants to keep this short. She is still not sure she wants to hear what he has to say.

Through an open door she sees toys piled untidily in a playpen, a hobby horse, lipstick, a worn powder compact, left open carelessly on a shelf. There is a faint odor of cheap perfume. There is a young wife and some children, here, too, she surmises. They must have been sent out in a hurry.

Malachy, whether he senses her unease or feels similarly pressed for time, gets down to business in a hurry. Perhaps the young wife knows nothing about this visit. He sits beside her on the sofa and says that he has something to show her. He picks up the large white envelope on the coffee table. He has some photographs for her. She shuffles through them, dull black-and-whites of a road. Why would she want to look at that? She frowns and stares up at him, inquiringly. "I don't understand," she says, which is only partly true. She looks at the other older, broader man, who sits opposite them in an armchair, watching with empty brown eyes.

Malachy asks her to look at the photos again, carefully. She shuffles reluctantly through them fast, once again. He explains that they were taken of the road where the accident took place. He makes the word "accident" sound as if it is in inverted commas.

She looks at his thin, fair face and wonders why he is telling her all of this. There is something light, insubstantial about him. What is his angle in all of this, revenge? She is not sure she trusts him.

"No skid marks, no rain," Malachy goes on, suggestively. "And Louis is no drinker, obviously." He had been his friend, this Malachy, and had his power-of-attorney, she remembers. Now he is turning on him.

The other man nods his dark head. "A surgeon," he says, by way of explanation, looking at his own large, strong hands, the gold signet ring.

"He is wearing a seat belt, she is not," Malachy goes on. He adds, "A history of violence, you must know about that. Bruises, black eyes. He was always beating her up."

She nods. She knows all of this. What does he want her to do? She has always known all of this, even while denying it to herself. She thinks of her mother saying to her sister, "You cannot marry an Afrikaner, they are just too emotional."

She remembers telephone calls from her mother. "Black-and-blue," her mother would say angrily. "I'm afraid he's going to shut her up in the sauna or drown her, out sailing."

"Oh, for goodness sake! Don't exaggerate, Mother," she would say, annoyed at being drawn into this.

Now she stares at the photographs and wants to turn back time, to hold onto her sister, take her in her arms and never let her go. How could she have turned her back on her?

She remembers the last time she saw her. It was in Geneva. "I don't want to go home at all. I'm afraid," her sister had said. But she had pushed her sister to do so, citing the children.

She feels her sister's presence now, vibrating in this small, ordinary room as a physical thing, a heat in her that is different from her own, something added. Why did she not help her? Why did her sister have to turn to this insubstantial man, who sits sweating on the sofa beside her? Why did she not admit the gravity of her sister's situation? Why, for God's sake, did her sister not protect herself? Why is she left now to deal with this?

She shakes her head at Malachy. She sighs and waves her hands helplessly. She says, "What can we do about this now? Can we prove it in a court of law?"

The other man, who has been sitting quietly in his armchair, leans forward and stubs out his cigarette in the ashtray on the coffee table, the tips of his fingers yellow with nicotine. He leans his head to one side slightly and tells her he knows one way to handle this kind of problem. She sits forward on her chair and looks inquiringly at Malachy, who explains that the man is a private detective. He has taken the liberty of asking him to come here today to meet her in the hope that justice may be done.

"I see," Kate says, looking at the man. Now that she knows he's a detective, she thinks he looks like a detective in films, which is the only place she has ever seen one before.

The detective removes a piece of tobacco from his tongue and coughs a smoker's cough. "Probably the only way to handle it," he says, rubbing his chin.

"What do you mean?" she asks, and all the air in the small room seems to have gone out of it. There is a pause.

He looks at her and says in a quiet, calm voice that the best way, perhaps the only way, to handle something of this kind would be to get rid of the husband. For a reasonable fee it could be accomplished quite smartly. He knows someone who would be happy to oblige.

"Oblige!" she says and stares at the detective.

She has the impression she has stepped into some sort of a thriller. The Venetian blinds in the small, low-ceilinged room are closed. She imagines she is in this man's office, his name on the pebbled glass of the door. He lights up another cigarette and blows out the smoke. Humphrey Bogart but not nearly so handsome, she thinks.

For a moment she considers the offer, seeing it in her mind's eye: Louis's removal, like a word deleted from a page, or a face cut out of a photograph. She thinks of her sister in the car that night, speeding toward the pole at the side of the road, of the moment of terror. Did she have time to think of her children, sleeping in their beds? Of what would happen to them?

But what if he were not deliberately responsible? And who is she to decide on the guilt or innocence of another? And even if he is? Surely he intended to take his own life, too? She wonders what her sister would have wanted her to do. If only she could tell her.

She looks at the detective and considers. Lines from her hours in the chapel at school come to her, "Vengeance is mine, saith the Lord." She shakes her head. "I'm afraid, I couldn't do something like that. My sister would never have wanted me to. I don't think it would be something I could live with."

He shrugs his shoulders and says it is, of course, entirely up to her. She just has to say the word and put up the cash. He lights up another cigarette, exhales smoke, and adds, "Though you might consider it seriously. A man who will kill once is capable of doing it again."

She rises then, fast. She wants to get out of here, away from these men with their talk of killing. She shakes their hands and says she will think all of this over. She steps out of the small, airless house into the fading light and tells Wilson to drive her back to Crossways.

Dusk falls, the last of the light glimmering in the tips of the jacarandas, as they draw near to the house. The sun sinks into nothingness. Approaching the white gates in the gloaming, she glimpses a flash of something white, a man, it seems to her, or is it a woman? in a white coat, going toward the gates. The figure is running along the road. Even in the distance and the half-light there is something familiar about its form, but she doesn't ask Wilson to stop the car to find out who it is, entering the garden.

XIII

H<small>E STANDS BEHIND THE JACARANDA</small> in the gloaming, watching the black Jaguar go up the driveway. He wonders where K.K. has been. All the time he was lying in his bed in the hospital he imagined her sitting in the garden with his children. Has she already been gadding around like her sister? He had insisted his wife be there every day at lunch when he came home. He wanted to know exactly what she was doing and whom she was seeing. He wanted to know what she was up to. He had even hired a private detective to follow her. In the end it had done no good.

There was always part of her that escaped him. Everything moved her, everyone's sufferings but his own. She never understood him. She never knew how to comfort him. She had hurt him. She had betrayed him with his friend, Malachy.

Is this sister as untrustworthy as his wife turned out to be? Has she been out stirring up trouble? Could she have been to see the police, perhaps? And what does she know about children, after all, about his children, never having had any of her own?

He slips along under the alley of jacarandas, approaching the house. He watches the car come to a stop. She gets out. She goes toward the front door, moving the way her sister did. She has the same light step, the head held high. From that distance and in the fading light, she might be her sister. He feels the same old blind rage rising in him. His dog, Rosie, comes out, too. She remains in the garden when K.K. enters the house, sniffing around. The dog comes running over to him and starts barking. Stupid dog. Doesn't even recognize her master. He gives her a kick and sends her sprawling.

He goes further up the driveway, staying under the trees. He waits in the shadows, watching the house. The lights are lit. The blue sky looks almost transparent, pierced with stars. He looks up at the bay window in the nursery, where his children must be sleeping. He imagines their faces, their arms and legs sprawled over the sheets with abandon. They hate to be covered, even on a cold night. He can always slip in the back door of the hospital, which is left open, should he lose his nerve. No one will have noticed his absence. At first all he wanted was some fresh air.

Now he is not so sure, not sure at all. Where has K.K. been? Who has she been seeing? Has she betrayed him as his wife did?

The trees protect him from being seen from the windows. He stares through their leafy barrier. After a while he is rewarded for his patience by the sight of Kate. She wanders out into the garden. She tilts her head back to look up at the night sky. Music from the open door rises and falls, losing itself in the hushing sound of the wind in the trees. The distant sound of traffic crosses the garden. It floats toward him. It makes the space seem vast. Darkness rolls in.

XIV

I T IS EIGHT-THIRTY, and the light is gone. K.K. has reentered the house. He undoes the buttons of his white coat. He leans against the jacaranda. He can hear footsteps on the path, quick, intermittent. A light flickers by the hedge near the tennis court, the lit tip of a cigarette. He smells the acrid smell of *dagga*. His breathing becomes shallow. He tells himself to relax. He drops his shoulders. To his left he sees a shape moving through the trees, catching the corner of his eye. He draws back against the tree and watches as the old colored gardener goes into the shed, carrying his tools, singing softly. He comes out, padlocking the door behind him.

Louis has been in that shed how many times? He would go in there to meet the old gardener and pay him for a *rook*. Also, he liked to drive the mini-tractor to mow the lawn. He even liked to weed the vegetable patch, as he had done for his mother, though he was never interested in flowers. Once, he dug up his mother-in-law's roses and planted pumpkins. "Much more useful, with all these servants in the house," he had said. What a furor there had been over that! He cannot help chuckling at the thought of it. Likewise the letter he once wrote to his mother-in-law on pink toilet paper! What a joke!

He liked to play hide-and-seek with the children in the damp darkness in the shed. He remembers chasing the little boy, Mark's friend, in there that evening. He remembers the high-pitched cries. There was the musty smell, the overturned flowerpots, the lawn mower. Grease dripped onto the dirt floor below. In the dim light the boy's face emerged from the shadows, the round head, the clear eyes, the dark hair, damp around the forehead. He pounced, catching him by his pink shirt, which hung out of his short, gray school-boy pants.

"Dr. Marais?" the high-pitched boy-voice came. He remembers when his own voice sounded like that. He remembers singing in the choir at the Dutch Reformed Church. He was a musical child. He remembers pumping the organ for his mother. Perhaps what he is in love with, what he cannot resist, is that lost boy of long ago, the boy he was never allowed to be. Is this what he has attempted to hold onto, this shadow of his own youth?

Their eyes met. The boy attempted a half-smile, polite, disarming, not yet afraid, just a little puzzled by an adult so caught up in a child's game. He was impelled to put his hands onto the boy's shoulders, as he had been impelled with the boy years ago in the locker room. No way to stop himself. Nothing could touch him at that moment. A crazy feeling of power. He rubbed slowly, harder and harder. His fingers lingered on the bones of the vertebrae. "Feel good, no?" he asked, though the boy only cast his gaze on the ground. He was sure the boy was really enjoying it, so much he shook and attempted to wriggle away.

Whatever the boy was feeling, he couldn't have stopped himself then, had he tried. He knew what he was doing was dangerous. He could hear the other children's cries. Someone was calling the boy, but he held him still. The risk made it even more irresistible. He has always been like this. There is irresistible excitement in the danger itself. He cannot help but choose moments like this, moments which release themselves from the flow of things, expand and become absolute. These are when he knows he will commit rash, unthinking acts.

He remembers the party when Marion came out and found him with Serge. His own birthday party. He knows he could not have chosen a worse moment to do what he did, but it was what made it the best. All his bloody relatives were in the house. Ouma and Oupa had come from the Great Karoo. All his brothers and sisters and their children were there. The children were jumping on the trampoline. He could hear their voices. Marion had made all the party food. She had cooked for days for his family, as she kept reminding him.

It was a clear, still night after a windy Highveld day. The clarity and stillness of the air seemed to have altered his perception. Or perhaps he had had a *rook*. But it wasn't that. The sizes, the distances between things around him were altered. The lawn looked larger, stretching on forever. The trees were huge against the sky. The jacarandas with their light flowers decorated the sky for him. With the family around him he was invulnerable, omnipotent. He was outside the laws of society, a million miles from everything. What Marion couldn't understand was that there was no choice, that it meant nothing at all.

In the shed his hands slipped upwards, circled the boy's neck. He watched himself do it. He told the boy what had to be done. He increased the pressure around the thin neck slightly, just enough to make him understand, just enough to make him do what he really wanted to do. He is convinced of that. He never wanted to hurt him. The boy lowered his head and took his aching flesh in his mouth. There was no way to stop it happening. He remembers the rush of relief. He remembers the way his breath came full again, his head light. He remembers the boy leaning over and choking into the dirt.

For a moment, under the trees in the darkness, he feels again the devouring shame, as he did when he heard about Pottie. He feels the shame like a choking for breath. Poor Pottie. They had taken his teaching away from him, his boys, something he had loved more than anything else. He had hung himself in his closet out of shame.

But he has learned not to think about that. He knows how to discard unwanted thoughts and feelings. Sometimes he is not quite certain this underground life of his exists at all. He never speaks of it, of course. It might be someone else's yellowed photographs from an old album. There are moments when he has been tempted to talk. But he knows not to divulge his secrets to anyone. He rarely thinks of them. He acts without thought, as if in a dream, or as if he were not there. He watches himself act as though it were someone else, or as though he is moved by a superior force.

His secret life seeps on beneath the smooth surface of his orderly existence: the doctor's life with its acts of mercy, its kindnesses, politeness, its tact, its struggle against death. Underneath is this secret stream gathering until it becomes irresistible. It erupts onto the surface from time to time. He knows this will happen again and again. There is no drawing back when it does, no choice.

Sometimes, though, it would surprise him, after being out all night, to be greeted by the nurses when he entered the hospital in the morning. Their liquid, admiring glances, their whispered, respectful assents to his orders. He would be surprised by the cups of coffee, offered with trembling hands, by the polite small talk. "Lovely day, Doctor, isn't it?" It amazed him that no one knew, no one could guess. Was it not visible somewhere in his eyes or his smile? Could they not see the special, silent places where he had lingered? Could they not smell the odor of damp and wet? He could smell them on himself, the park benches in the gloaming, the dark, malodorous alleys behind the bar in Hillbrow, the stink of urine and beer, the men's toilets. Surely there was something in his expression and gestures that would give him away? But no one noticed. No one dreamed that he lived a double life.

Oh, they expected there was something going on with the prettier nurses or his secretary. Even Marion had suspected his secretary, the earnest, efficient Gill, a wealthy Jewish girl with red hair who worked for love, who adored him. He is surprised she has not been to visit. The handsome doctor, the pretty nurses, the efficient secretary: a classic soap-opera scenario. It was unavoidable. Occasionally, he had complied out of generosity. Or out of lethargy. He had allowed certain things to be done to him, quick, meaningless fumbles, breasts brushed against his arm, toes which had sought him out under the table, knees pressed against his. He had been grateful for these anonymous acts with one or two of the night nurses, his mind elsewhere, on someone else, something more exciting. It was oddly comforting in its normality.

There are women whom he finds attractive, after all, but not in that helpless, irresistible, secret way. It was the women who would sometimes seek him out late at night on the ward or at a hospital party. Sometimes, when they had had a few drinks, they came to him, the handsome doctor. They would sidle up and smile at him. They would flash him a damp, despairing glance. He would let them lead him into some dim place. He would let them press him up against the coats on a bed. He would submit to their sighs, the hot, beery breath, the soft kisses, the whispered words of desire. He would lie flat on his back. He would fold his arms behind his head. He would allow them to caress his sex with their sticky fingers, their damp mouths. Sometimes he let them, if they begged, slip it into their damp, aching flesh.

He has always liked women who do not resemble his fair, flabby, excitable mother. He likes women with broad shoulders and not too many words. He likes good swimmers with a little fur on their upper lip. He likes phlegmatic women who don't show off, not the screamers, the screechers, or the babblers. He prefers women who give you little trouble. He likes the quiet ones who can unexpectedly turn out to be passionate, as Marion could.

When she had screwed off the top of the bed post and thrown it at him, a stake in his heart, it had excited him. She had known it would. He had given her a good thrashing that time, which he is certain she enjoyed. He likes women excited enough, or at least willing to work to get his cock erect. He likes them to get down on their knees and beg and sweat and grovel. *Asseblief, asseblief.* He wants them to work to make him tumescent, strong as a staff. He likes women who, if he half shuts his eyes, he can imagine are boys. He likes women not too far from his fantasies of men, like his dead wife, or perhaps, his dead wife's sister.

Of course, in the particular case of the boy in the shed, he had run straight home to tell his Ma. And this Ma, an exception, had believed him. She had not just believed him but wanted to make a fuss, a scandal. Silence somewhere along the line was what usually ensued. Silence is his salvation. It never ceases to surprise him. Mostly people prefer silence to scandal, to the trouble, the work involved. Silence is in everyone's interest, after all. Silence is a necessary part of civilization.

But this woman was stubborn. A lawyer, one of those women who like to cause trouble.

He wonders if K.K. is of the same sort. Where has she been today? Suddenly, standing in the hot night garden, leaning against the jacaranda tree, he knows he hates her. She is an intruder, a usurper. She has come to take his place with his own children. He wants her out of the way. He imagines she's an unhappy, lonely woman. She lives out her spinster life on her own in small, dark rooms in Paris. He thinks of her as a rat. She burrows underground. She has come here to suck on his babies, on him. Why does she not go back from whence she came, where she belongs? She is too thin, as is the lawyer, no doubt. Most probably, the lawyer would have liked to do what he did with the boy. Why else did she think it necessary to press charges, to wreck his life? She must have gone to another lawyer to have her letter drafted, or perhaps she drafted it, herself. He has always hated lawyers.

He feels a twitching in his legs, a sort of tremor in the muscles. He's not used to standing for so long. He's been lying on his back for weeks. He would like to rest for a moment now. He half-closes his eyes. The trees are swinging around him.

Reluctantly, he leaves the shadows. He lingers to look back at the red brick house with its inviting lights. He picks a few flowers in the dark, as he goes along the driveway, his flowers, after all. He takes them with him. He looks at them under the lamp light and then decides they are not worth keeping. They look damaged, and he sees ants crawling on them. He discards them in the road. The family is not keeping the place up the way it should be kept up in his absence. He will not easily relinquish his rightful place here with his children, to this woman.

XV

"ARE YOU SURE YOU FEEL UP TO IT?" the young nurse asks nervously. She is twisting something green around in her fingers, a paper clip, perhaps.

"I miss them so much," he says as pathetically as possible. He is sitting in his chair by the window in his dark-blue silk dressing gown. He crosses his legs. He lets the gown fall back from his leg. It is early morning, and the heat is coming up. He can see a tick bird pecking at the lawn.

He lowers his eyelashes mournfully. He does miss his children, though he had felt it might have been better if all of them had gone together that night.

He had seriously considered taking the three children along, too. He had stared at them lying on the beds, the waxy faces, the plump arms, the little fingers stretched out stiffly, as if they were already half-dead. For what would become of them? What will become of them, now, with this sister, who is probably just as unreliable as the mother, and the grandmother who is half drunk all the time, and the grasping great-aunt?

He felt they would be lucky to be done with it all. No more worries, no more lies, no more hiding, no more striving, no more things you want to be that you never will. He had thought they would all go together, as his colleague, an anesthetist, had done, gassing his whole family, though he had botched the job, too, and only killed two of the children and the wife.

The nurse licks her thick lips and says, "I do understand how you would want to be with your children, Dr. Marais, and you do seem much improved. Perhaps we can arrange something. I will speak to Dr. Walsh." She smiles, her head cocked slightly to one side. Definitely not his type, too blond, too emotional.

"Why don't you just call and tell them I want to visit this Sunday? Dr. Walsh might just delay things unduly, with all his talk and ridiculous tests," he says, staring at her.

"This Sunday? So soon? I think we ought to let Dr. Walsh have a little look at you first," she says, coming nearer to him, propping herself up on the end of the bed.

"We don't need a half-brained psychiatrist. They're all half mad themselves. You must know that, smart as you are. You have a real doctor, here, a surgeon," he replies and grins— the old grin, lifts a hand to scratch the back of his head, lets the sleeve of his gown slip down his arm and flexes his muscles slightly.

She is taking it all in. She blushes. She laughs. "Well, yes, of course, Dr. Marais."

He rises and goes toward her. He puts his hand on her shoulder, squeezes gently, touches the back of her neck as he speaks. He bends down, speaks softly, "Tell them I'm fine, hey? Tell them I'm *compos mentis*. Tell them you'll bring me yourself. You got a car, no? Tell them you'll drive me there and back. Tell them what you like. Tell them to go to hell." He wonders where his car keys are.

She flushes, lifts her head up, and smiles back at him. She says, "I can see you are going to be leaving us soon. I'm going to miss you," and lowers her eyelashes mournfully, leaning up against him. Not one brain in her pretty head, he thinks, letting his fingers slip through the buttons of her blouse, touch her nipple, and give it a twist.

"Whatever you think," she breathes, pressing her hot body up against him. "Whatever you want."

It wasn't a lack of brains with Marion.

Sometimes all he wanted was to get a rise out of her. He just wanted to get her to react to him. He wanted her to raise her voice, lose her temper, and shout back something obscene. He often felt invisible in her presence. She would blink her dark eyes blankly at him, as though he were not there. Mostly she would just sigh or her soft mouth would turn down slightly at the corners. Sometimes, infuriatingly, she would say something in French, which he does not speak. Or she might just turn her back. Often she would be busy with someone else's problems. She would rush off to help with someone else's sick child. Once in a while, he had been able to goad her to strike back. She had even bought herself a water gun, but he had simply turned that onto her. He had to laugh at that. They had both ended up laughing, that time.

At the last minute he had decided not to take the children, already asleep in their beds, limbs sprawled across the sheets: too much trouble. He must have buckled his seat belt. And then he must have turned the car wheel slightly away from the pole. But he doesn't remember that moment or what happened then.

She was already half asleep, that evening. There was no other way. Once she had betrayed his trust, wanted to leave him, he had no choice. He had intended to go with her, after that letter, which would have ruined his career. When she left, he had wanted to die. He had tried that once before, unsuccessfully.

XVI

"**N**O WAY WE CAN REFUSE, of course," her mother says. She is knitting again, sitting out in the garden in the shade of the oak tree in an upright chair beside her sister, who knits, too. They are both wearing cream blouses and cream pleated skirts. Perspiration glistens on their pale foreheads. It is a hot late December afternoon, the height of summer, the poinsettias in bloom, the sky white with heat and already turning a garish orange around the edges.

Kate says, "I don't think it's a good idea. He is likely to upset the children." She is sitting barefooted beside them in her sister's straw hat and one of her sister's sleeveless summer dresses. She has not brought enough clothes, or had time to go shopping, or expected she would have stayed so long.

Besides, she likes to wear her sister's clothes, though they are a little loose on her, just as she liked to wear the same dresses when they were children. She holds them to her face, she hunts for her sister's odor like an animal. She breathes her in. She misses her sister with a deep, lonely ache: the sharing of dresses, shoes, gloves—"Here, take mine, darling," her sister would say, if Kate lost something; the sharing of jokes about their mother, their aunt, Uncle Charles, everything; the half-admiring, half-exasperated sister remarks.

She looks at Mark and his two sisters, playing solemnly together, at some distance from the grown-ups. She envies them their game, their closeness to one another, their imaginary world, even their squabbles. At least they have one another. A sister is supposed to be with you all your life.

The children are playing funeral in the flowers. Deidre has wrapped one of her dolls in a white table napkin and covered it with flowers and carries it, both hands stretched out before her, like a bier. Lydia has the silver candlesticks from the dining-room table, which she is swinging like bells in her small hands, flowers in a wreath around her head, and Mark walks bolt upright behind his sisters, playing the minister in the procession with one of Kate's dark-colored scarves draped over his head and shoulders, muttering some kind of incantation, totally absorbed by his game.

Dottie knits on relentlessly in the heat, the steel needles clicking loudly, ferociously. She says, "How about the father, he is their father, whatever you may think of him. What did the nurse say?"

"Just that he wishes to come for a visit on Sunday. He won't stay long. She'll bring him and pick him up after tea," her mother says. "I don't see how we can refuse to see him."

Dottie says, "We should thank God he is well enough to come and wants to be with his children. It is his rightful place, after all."

"Did you ask the nurse how he is in his mind?" Kate asks her mother.

Her mother puts down her knitting. She says, "According to the nurse he's much better. *Compos mentis*, was how she put it, I believe. She thinks it would be good for him."

'"Good for him, but I still feel he shouldn't come here," Kate says, rising and walking back and forth in the grass, swiping at it with her bare feet. "Could the children not visit him in the hospital? Wouldn't that be better?"

Her mother turns to her and says, "Perhaps we should just let him stay here for a while and see how it goes. The children would be happy to have him, don't you think? He would take care of them, after all. Whatever you can say about him, he does love them, and they love him."

"I wouldn't," she says warningly.

The two elderly women sit with their knitting in the shadows, their faces full of worry, grief, fatigue, and the desire to be free of any responsibility. "Children need a father, however imperfect," her aunt ventures, without looking up at her, adding, "Neglect is the worst abuse."

How can she argue with that? She holds her straw hat in one hand. It is only making her feel hotter. Though the sun is setting, it is not cooling off. She says, "There has been such a history of violence," but she feels it is all hopeless.

Her mother sighs and says she knows. It is most unfortunate that he has such a bad temper, is such an impulsive man. "You never know what he is going to do next," she says in a loud voice. She continues. She would have chosen another father, almost any other father, for her grandchildren, another husband for her daughter. She says Marion was always running to her with a black eye, but what can they do about it now? Has the father not been punished enough?

Kate thinks of Malachy's detective and wonders whether she should give him a ring, after all. She wonders just how reliable he is, if he is to be trusted. What has happened to her sister's money in Switzerland? She wonders, after all, if he were right. Could he have taken advantage of her sister financially and otherwise? She remembers her sister coming in late to the hotel room in Geneva the night they stayed there, her cheeks flushed. She thinks of her own words to her sister in Rome: "Seize the day. Take a lover, for goodness sake, " when her sister told her of her husband's infidelity. She knows she had followed her advice. She had gone on to Turkey and written back to her about her lover.

"He looks like a mixture between Donatello's and Michelangelo's David," her sister had written to her. She thinks of how her sister's husband had found a letter from the lover and had slit his veins, lying at the top of the stairs and calling the children and the servants around him, as her sister had written to her afterwards.

"You better watch out you are not stung by a bee, walking barefooted in the grass like that," her aunt says, glancing up from her knitting. She adds, "If he's better, they won't keep him in the hospital much longer. He will have to go somewhere eventually. Where's he going to go?"

She wants to say that prison might be a good place, but what if she were wrong?

They had come together, her sister and the accountant, to Geneva to steal back money which was her sister's, after all, money that her husband had taken from their joint account and put into his own. They had, thanks to the accountant, stolen the money back and opened an account for her sister. She wonders again what has happened to the money now. She thinks of her aunt stealing money from her mother's handbag.

Her mother says, "We should avoid the scandal, for the children's sake. Keep their names out of the paper. They have already suffered enough, surely. Besides, what can you actually prove in a case like this?"

Her aunt adds, "And who is going to take care of the children, when you go on home?"

She bends down, slips on her sandals, and walks toward the house. As she goes, she overhears her aunt say, "I just wish she would go home, now. She's just making trouble." Her mother does not reply.

How can her mother let her aunt speak about her like this behind her back? she thinks. She wishes that she could just leave. Rene has called from the South of France. He is at the farmhouse on his own. He sounded confused and angry. His work was not going well. He says he cannot write without her. He tells her he realizes now how dependent he has become on her, not only in his life but in his work. The two things are inextricably linked.

"You mean poetry and sex?" she said.

He told her he feels she is not only his muse, but also his best reader. She understands his aspirations toward a purer poetry. She knows his sources.

And it is true that she has read Rene Char, Eluard, and Aragon in order to understand his work. Perhaps she has understood him better than she thought. Perhaps she has been able to explain his work better than he can, himself. But how can she just leave these children now?

She is thinking of her visit to the accountant's house, and what she saw on the way home. She has the impression Louis might have been lurking in the garden. She wonders what to say about all of this to her mother. Is this the moment to speak up? Why had her sister not spoken up more clearly, herself? How could her sister have let things go so far?

XVII

I T WAS A SUMMER EVENING, and she was visiting out here, the aunt from France, the one who translated other people's books and who told stories in the sauna to the children. She was photographing them all once again. "Say cheese," she said.

Her sister stood legs apart, with the older ones on either side and the new baby in her arms. She was in her loose, blue, linen dress, her stomach swelling gently from her pregnancies. Her shape had become slightly fuller, and it was hard to decide if she was pregnant again or had not yet recovered from her last pregnancy. The veins in her legs were a faint blue, her skin was dusted with fine freckles, her soft curls, thinned, the teeth, slightly blue.

Looking at her sister with the three children, Kate thought that all of the Kempden women suffered from excess. Their Mother's was first food, the blood sucked from steaks, the drippings soaked up with dry pieces of bread, the hard-boiled eggs staining her lips yellow, and now it was drink and the many and varied pills which Dottie conveniently provided for her to swallow by the fistful, with the help of the doctor in the family.

Her own excess was now her work, her endless hours of translating, the difficult French books she struggled with, sitting in Paris without looking out her window at the Pantheon across the park and only at the paper in her typewriter, the book beside her, or the dictionary. She worked constantly now, since becoming in some demand by the French intelligentsia to translate their work. She had translated some stories by Michel Tournier which had been published by Bloomsbury and praised highly. Recently she had branched out to do a translation of an Italian novel by Elsa Morante which the *Times Literary Supplement* had described as, "A lovely moving book, translated with elegance and economy, delicately powerful."

Her sister's excess was pregnancy. She loved being pregnant, so that she did not have to prove anything to anyone. She could linger in the shade of a jacaranda with her book, dreaming baby dreams. She dreamed of baby clothes, booties, cream baby vests with the drawstring neck, cream baby viyella nightdresses with embroidered bibs, and big blue-and-white English baby prams and cradles like the ones from the fairy tales they had read as children, with ruffled skirts and veils falling down over the baby's soft, pink face. Her husband encouraged her in these baby dreams.

Her sister was drunk on babies, as if she craved them like a drug. She needed a new one every eighteen months, or was it that she had them thrust upon her? Kate wonders now, to end the quarrels and bring her husband back?

On that visit out there her sister was recovering from her last pregnancy, still staggering slightly when she rose to greet her, wearing a cotton cardigan that dragged around her knees, her hand to her back. Her white breasts were swollen and full of milk, the bright, white skin stretched and scarred. Its color, once glowing with light and life, looked dull and clouded, as though these three births in rapid succession had drained it away. She lay placidly in her room with the shutters down in the afternoons, sweating, her new baby on her breast, her spent curls clotted and clinging to her damp forehead, a pillow propping up her still swollen belly. "Never again, I will never do this," she swore.

But it seemed she could not stop. She wanted six, ten, a thousand babies. She wanted to be permanently pregnant.

A child was always slipping down her hip, or, clinging, arms slung around her neck, head at her breast. A toddler always leaned against her leg, her skirt crumpled in his fist. "Here, hold this one for a sec," Marion said to her, pressing something warm and fragrant and as light as a plume against her heart.

Now the children scattered around the big garden like rose petals blown about by the wind. They ran through the garden in white shorts and dresses with sleeves like wings, barefooted, bareheaded—"They wont keep their shoes or their hats on," her sister said, lifting her hands helplessly. The strong sun burned the delicate skin on their arms and legs crimson. Their noses peeled, the soft pink skin exposed. Always thirsty, their lips chapped, tongues hanging out like puppies, panting, they rushed into the big, cavernous kitchen to swing open the refrigerator door for lemonade, cokes, or soda water or just ice which John crushed by wrapping it in a towel and beating it against the wall.

The children flitted back and forth among the shadows and light like bats. Half naked, their feet stained red with mud, their cheeks a hectic scarlet, their foreheads damp, they were prone to high fevers and fits. The baby had nightmares, woke screaming in the night, until Lydia took her into her bed. They swallowed things, put beads up their noses, objects in their small orifices to be extracted, smelly and damp, by Louis, the busy doctor, who rushed home between one operation and the next.

They dropped off walls, tumbled out of bed, slipped off branches, breaking bones. They slid on Crossway's cold tiled floor, bruising their pink skin. Plum-colored bruises stained their tender skins and red welts marked their backs like a belt.

"You just have to look at them, and they bruise," Marion said.

Watching them, Kate felt that Marion had an embarrassment of riches with her three delicious children with their little fat legs, plump cheeks, soft, fragrant skins. Sometimes Kate, too, longed for someone warm, soft, and loving on her lap.

When she had arrived out here, that year, the older children ran to her begging for stories, games of make-believe. She lay on the top bunk in the sauna, and her sister lay with the children beneath her. "I'm coming to eat you up," Kate growled and stuck her fingers through the slats and waved them about.

"Coming to beat us," Lydia said, kicking her heels and pressing her naked body to the floor, covering her eyes with her fists. "To beat us hard with your belt," Mark said. "To scrub at our skin with the scrubbing brush when we are in the bath, and to make us do sit-ups because we are too, too disgustingly fat," the plump Mark said and shook until his teeth clacked together.

"It's too hot in here for them. Outside all of you. Outside you go, I said," Marion, lying on the lower slats, cried, her cheeks damp with sweat or was it tears?

XVIII

I T WAS HER SISTER who was called on at the end of class to recite a few lines of poetry in French for Mademoiselle, the French teacher, who wore orange lipstick to match her orange hair, which was swept up in a dramatic chignon. The teacher would make her sister come and stand in front of the class to recite Baudelaire's *Mon enfant, ma soeur, songe a la douceur,* or one of Victor Hugo's moving poems or those lovely lines of Mallarme's: *le vierge, le vivace et le bel aujourd'hui.* She recited well with much expression in a low but melodious voice. She wasn't shy or self-conscious, as Kate herself would have been. As a girl, she could never stand up in public to speak, though she has learned over the years to read her translations to an audience, trembling a little, but in a clear voice. Now she can answer questions about the work she translates, thanks to the impression it is someone else speaking through her. She hears herself from a distance saying, "Difficulty and paradox are the essence of the work."

Strangely, because her sister had never been to France, or only briefly, she had hardly any accent at all, and her words must have brought back Mademoiselle's own adolescence in the Midi, because they sometimes made her cry. She would see Mademoiselle wipe away a tear surreptitiously.

Kate remembers that moment in her own life when everything seemed possible, when she and her sister had planned to go abroad together. And indeed, her sister might have been a teacher, or an actress, a film star, or a singer of songs. Instead, she had married Louis Marais immediately after she had finished her degree.

She remembers what her mother said when her sister first announced her intention of marrying: "Over my dead body will you marry a Boer." She has always wondered if it was one of the reasons why she went ahead and did it. Her sister had her stubborn side when she believed in what she was doing.

"You can't help loving someone," she had said to her mother, when her mother protested. "But he comes from such a different background, darling," their mother said mildly. She must have known it was useless to protest.

XIX

S HE IS LYING THERE with a cool cloth over her forehead, when she hears the knock on the door. It is Sunday morning, in December, the day their father is to come to visit his children. When she told them, they said nothing at this news, so that she thought they might not have understood.

Now she has retreated to the bathroom and is stretched out in the big bath, her hair caught up on her head, reading her book, the Anita Brookner her sister had been reading, when the children come to find her. "*Kskatie, Kskatie,* can we come in?" they ask, opening the door, peering in. She sees the three faces through the steam.

"Can we come in the bath with you?" the oldest asks, entering boldly. Deidre sits down on the bathmat on the floor, legs apart, as she must have done many times before with her mother. She has opened up the cupboard under the sink, and is pulling things out, the soap, the toilet paper, the pills.

"Don't touch the pills, darling," she says anxiously, hanging half out of the bath. What a responsibility these children are, she thinks. Why is her sister not here to care for them?

"We want to come in the bath with you, *Kskatie*," the eldest persists, adding, "Mummy always let us come in the bath with her."

"All right then," Kate says, moved by the boy's words. She folds up her legs obligingly and covers her breasts shyly with the washcloth. The middle one has already called her Mummy by mistake and had to be corrected. "Darling, I love you very much, but I'm not your Mummy, I'm afraid, and I never can be."

Lydia lifts the little one's dress over her head, and takes off her pants. Kate reaches over the edge of the bath and lifts Deidre up and holds her on her lap in the water, her head leaning back against her knees, shutting her eyes and lolling on Kate's lap in the warm water, happy, almost asleep. The other two undress fast and climb in, the eldest huddled over in front, his back to Kate, and the middle one crouched behind her back.

She remembers how she and her sister would climb in the bath together, her sister in front, her own legs around her sister's waist, going around the big bath, "going overseas," splashing water all over the floor.

She leans forward and traces the blue welts across the boy's back with her finger. "Whatever happened here?" she asks before she realizes what such marks must mean.

He says nothing, but his sister reports from behind Kate's back. "That's from when he was bad, and Daddy had to use the belt on him."

She feels a sharp fear contract her stomach muscles. "Did Mummy know about this?" she asks.

"Oh yes," Lydia replies, "She had to take him to the hospital, because he couldn't wake up."

"Wake up?" she asks. How could her sister have let this happen? Why had she not told anyone? Why had she not left this monster! She has a strong urge to hit her sister, to slap her across the face, and tell her to wake up.

"Lydia means I was unconscious," the boy says in a small, guilty, adult voice.

"But you won't be bad again, will you Mark?" Lydia says to her brother who says nothing.

XX

JOHN OPENS THE DOOR for the *baas* and the nurse when they knock on the door, loudly, just as he did for the two policemen who came at midnight with the news of the accident and death. He is always the one who opens the front door, and thus he is the one who knows what happens in this house before anyone else does. He stands there, very upright, at his full height, in his starched white uniform with the blue sash, which hangs from one shoulder to the waist. He opens the door to the *baas* in silence.

They have arrived early, before John has been able to retreat for a rest, and while he was still washing up the luncheon things by hand in the pantry, and before Mrs. Kempden and her sister have come downstairs from their naps. The other servants are resting in their quarters, but John, who was paying attention and hears everything, has heard the car coming up the driveway, and has called out to *Kskatie* to inform her of this coming, and to tell her to gather up the children, and to warn them that their father has arrived.

They have spent all morning dressing up in their best shorts and smocked dresses, their pants to match, their brown lace-ups and patent-leather shoes, and John has gone upstairs and helped with these preparations in order to make sure they are accomplished properly. The boy has chosen the blue shorts with a white shirt, and Lydia, the red sun dress, and Deidre a pale pink one, with pink rosebuds, because it is the same color as *Kskatie's*. The children have chosen *Kskatie's* dress and her shoes as well, she has told him proudly.

He has been asked to find lost objects, and he has given an extra polish to the children's shoes for good measure, though he has already polished them once. He has hunted for the children's long socks, which no one else can find, as they haven't been worn for a while. He has been asked to look for them because Daddy likes them in long socks, the little ones have told him. Though he is half-blind, he is the only one in the house who knows where to find missing things, where everything is.

He has heard the boy ask *Kskatie* to wash his hair carefully and to French-braid Lydia's gold locks and tie the braid with a red ribbon. Even Deidre, who doesn't seem to have much memory of her father, has asked to have her hair done in two little bunches, and he has gone to find the extra elastics in the box for this operation, so that her hair sticks straight out on either side of her pale face, the way she wished it to, and made him chuckle at her and flip the soft bunches with the tips of his fingers like the ends of paint brushes, which she told him not to do. He shook his head and laughed at her and flipped her bunches again. He lifted her onto his back and pretended she was a rider and rushed around the nursery to make her giggle.

John has had the cook prepare Granadilla cake with white icing, one of the *baas's* favorites, and the sandwiches of anchovy paste he likes, too, on a bed of finely chopped lettuce. The house smells of baking cake, and there are flowers in the vases, and everything is in order.

Now *Kskatie* stands in the lounge with the children at her side in the early afternoon light, as he ushers in the young nurse who holds the *baas* by one hand, to the top of the steps which go down into the sunken room.

"Here we are," he hears the nurse say, cheerfully, in a loud, false nurse voice. She has the little blue cape around her shoulders, which they usually wear, and he imagines that her starched cap trembles on her head. Her crepe-soled shoes glimmer spotless, he is glad to see, and he notices how she attempts to hold the *baas's* hand, but he breaks free of her immediately and descends the steps fast, going toward his children, arms outstetched.

"*My kinders!*" he cries out exultantly.

But the children do not seem to move. They appear to be frozen in place, and they do not leave *Kskatie's* side. They stand so stiffly, it seems to him, they look like small soldiers at attention, waiting to do battle, awkwardly clinging onto their aunt's hands and skirt. The *baas*, too, stands uncertainly before his children, with, John imagines, surely, though he cannot actually see them, tears in his eyes. *Kskatie*, moved, it seems to him though he does not know by what—a desire to get this over with, perhaps, or by the *baas's* distress, or by the ancient politeness of all women, particularly these women in this house who seem to have the sentiment that all men, or at any rate all white men, need to be assisted in the domain of feelings, or perhaps by the thought of her own father, lost when she was the same age as the boy—gives the children a little push and offers them up to this father, just as, he who remembers everything, remembers her mother once offering her and her sister to the *baas*, like a bunch of wild flowers, at the party when they met, so long ago. *Kskatie* says, "Say hallo to your father, children."

They go up solemnly and in silence to lift a cheek to be kissed, and the *baas* bends down and kisses them. Only the little one stands uncertainly looking up at him and then back at *Kskatie*.

The nurse, on the steps, says, "I'll leave you now, with your lovely family, Dr. Marais."

Kskatie calls out, "You will fetch him after tea, please?"

He imagines that Louis glares at her, and that she feels the strength of his amber gaze.

The nurse nods and, surely, casts a last, tender, teary glance over her shoulder at her patient, as she goes up the steps and out of the lounge with a mournful squeak of her shoes. He smells her odor of talcum powder and soap and panic, which lingers in the air, and hears the car revving up and crunching the gravel of the driveway, and he wonders if this foolish young woman will remember to come and fetch the *baas* on time, and what will happen if she does not.

Unasked, the *baas* sits down on the sofa's yellow silk cushions, in his khaki safari suit. He leans back and spreads his arms out on either side, as if he has never been away, and John hears him pat the cushions hard on either side of him, cushions that he has plumped up that morning with care.

He thinks of how he has risen each day for so many years before dawn in his small windowless room, and warmed his *putu* on the coal fire, and begun polishing the furniture in this room for these white people. He has piled up all the furniture in the center of this room, to polish every inch of this parquet floor at dawn, daily. He knows no one notices if he does not polish every piece of furniture to a high shine and every inch of the parquet floor, but he does it for himself and for his illustrious ancestors, who were such diligent and hard-working and such brave people, and for this widow-woman, his *Nkosi,* and her children, to whom he has promised his allegiance and his love, long ago, and who rely on him to think for himself and do what needs to be done and also, he admits to himself, he polishes out of long habit, so that sometimes he cannot imagine doing anything otherwise.

Now the *baas* tells his children to come and sit beside him, and, slowly and obediently, the older two climb up and sit quietly on either side of him, legs dangling, crossed neatly at the ankles in the long socks he had found at the bottom of a drawer. Even the youngest, encouraged, he supposes, by a nod from *Kskatie,* finally follows her brother and sister and is clambering up beside her brother, when her father reaches out suddenly and lifts her up onto a knee, where she sits stiffly, unsmiling, her straight white hair sticking out on either side of her lowered face in the bunches that look like paint brushes. The *baas's* white-gold hair falls over his forehead, and he grins at them. *Kskatie* hovers beside John, where he stands by the door, which leads into the corridor and then into the kitchen, watching.

The *baas* says to his son, "You have lost a tooth. Is that the first one you have lost?"

"Actually, Daddy, it's the fifth," the boy says politely and probably points obligingly, showing off the space between the two front teeth.

"Of course! Of course it is! What am I thinking?" his father laughs and tickles his plump tummy. The child draws back from him. "And did the mouse bring you some money?" he asks.

The boy nods, and when his father asks how much, he informs him proudly he received a rand.

"Generous mouse! Sounds like tooth inflation to me," his father says. "In my day it used to be a tickie, hey John?" Perhaps he looks up at John and *Kskatie,* and she must be smiling at the child, for she is unlikely to be smiling at her brother-in-law. She says, and he hears her voice tremble, "Mother thought we should all have tea outside? I'll tell her you are here."

The *baas* does not reply to this. He has no interest in tea and he has no interest in his mother-in-law. He is whispering something in Lydia's ear that John does not understand, and she is probably looking up at him as if fascinated, like a chicken looking at a snake, John imagines. *Kskatie* follows him into the kitchen and stands before him uselessly at the kitchen table, where he sits down and takes up his polishing again. She offers to carry out the cups, the splendid white cake, and the tea sandwiches, which have been prepared and are under the netting to prevent flies, but they are both listening to the children.

He hears Lydia say, "*Kskatie* is sleeping in your room now, Daddy."

"Oh, she is, is she," the *baas* responds.

XXI

H<small>E FELT IT FROM THE MOMENT</small> he entered the house in his khaki safari suit, with the ridiculous nurse holding his hand. He was floating a few feet from the floor. He swaggered inside his front door. He caught a glimpse of his handsome face in the mirror over the chest. He saw the white-blond hair on the forehead, the strong thrust of the chin, the light eyes. He saw the kist and the telephone in the stairwell, as they were in his dreams. With the front door open there was sunlight in the hall. Nothing could touch him, now that he was back home. He pulled his hand from the nurse's. He broke free and rushed down the stairs to his *kinders*.

Now he sits in the vast, sunlit garden with the cup of tea on his lap. He has not come back to earth. He still feels lit up with a kind of crazy assurance. He feels a sense of unlimited power, of invulnerability. Not even the children's blank stares or the disapproving glances of the women have taken the feeling from him. On the contrary. He hovers up here, a few feet from the ground. He surveys the scene. He has brought forth the sun. He has conjured up the tennis court. He has made the morning glory grow up the wire. He has brought forth the pool, the smooth lawn, all the flowers, the jacarandas, the oak, even old John standing with stiff dignity in his starched white uniform and blue sash behind the trestle table under the oak tree. It is all his creation.

He knows the danger of such moods. They have dogged him all his life. He feels nothing can touch him. He is at an immense distance from these people. It was how he felt that night in the car with his wife. He feels reckless, out of control. He knows that sooner or later he will say something, do something rash. He knows he will strike out blindly.

He knows they are all aware of his mood. They sense his rebellious excitement. They watch him closely, fear in their eyes. Even the dog cowers at a distance, afraid. Their fear encourages him. John eyes him warily as he shuffles across the lawn and passes around the cake again. He starts to pass around the teapot, to fill up the cups, but K.K. rises. She takes the pot from him. "I'll do it, John." The old man cannot see a thing. They should send him home. What are they thinking?

The stilted conversation has halted in the heat. There is the stillness of the hot summer afternoon. There are the crickets, and the sound of the water falling over the wall, and the maddening clicking of Aunt Dottie's needles. That woman could knit in her sleep. Julia lifts her cup from her knee. She says, "Another cup of tea, Louis? You look awfully hot, dear. Kate, fill his cup," but he demurs.

He sits in a straight-backed wicker chair. He sweats in his khaki safari suit and his Gucci loafers. He wipes the sweat from his brow with the back of his sleeve. He watches his children. They have dressed them up as if they were going to church. They are like three dolls set on the low branch of a tree; the boy in the middle in his ridiculous blue shorts and frilled shirt, and the two girls on either side, their full skirts, the pink and the red, spread wide. They swing their feet in the long white socks and lace-ups and black patent-leather shoes, slowly, slowly. They swing back and forth. They are all eating large slices of the cook's Granadilla cake. They stare at him as if he were a stranger, as though they have never seen him before. The crumbs fall onto the ground around them in the grass. Birds peck at them.

He cannot bear to see his children looking like someone else's, to see them all scrubbed and dressed up like stuffed dolls. Each time he looks at them, he feels a surge of exaltation and the bitterness of having to rein it in. He cannot bear the thought of going back to the hospital, of being separated from them again. The unfairness of it maddens him. They belong to him.

He feels the rage of frustrated power build. He cannot sit here for another moment in the heat and the silence with these dreadful women. They all glance at him disapprovingly, fearfully. This was always a house of women, of sisters, of too many sisters.

K.K. sits beside her mother in his wife's straw hat and her sleeveless summer dress. What is she doing in them? What right does she have? The pink enamel bracelet on her wrist, the good one from Hermés, must be his wife's as well. How dare she just help herself! What has her role been over the years? What advice did she give her sister on that trip to Rome? What has she been doing since she has been out here but stirring up trouble.

Kate looks at her watch. She speaks in that clipped schoolmarm voice, his wife's voice. She talks to her mother, to his children, not to him. She speaks as though he were not there. She has not even shaken his hand or said, "Good afternoon." She doesn't look him in the eye.

"Perhaps we should all go inside now. Daddy will have to go back to the hospital soon. It is after four o'clock," she says.

The summer day is hotter than ever. A haze of heat shimmers in the air. John shimmers in his white uniform. He stands very upright watching them in silence under the oak tree with the tea things. The children shimmer, too. They jump down obediently from the branch. They abandon the remains of their cake on the table. They come towards K.K. and clutch her hands. The little one holds onto her skirt. What is K.K. doing in his wife's place in his house with his children?

Some part of him goes cold, but in another part he is exultant. Time stops dead while he stands and stares at Kate across a distance of perhaps two feet. He stares at her and spits out, "Daddy doesn't intend to go back to the hospital."

K.K. speaks in his wife's calm voice, "I'm afraid you will have to go back to the hospital, Louis. I'm going to call the nurse to make sure she comes for you now."

He glares at her. He sees the older women looking up at him nervously. Dottie has even stopped knitting. Her mouth hangs open. They are watching him, waiting to see what he will do. He feels he can do anything. Nothing can touch him.

He looks at his children. The three faces lift toward him. He sees his son's big dark eyes, the plump, pale cheeks. He sees his daughter's fancy plait with the red bow at the end, and the absurd bunches sticking out on either side of the little one's face. They have scraped her hair into bunches, goddamn it.

He moves fast. His spirit acts in spite of himself. He picks up the little one and swings her aloft. Her hair flies. The patent-leather shoes fly. She is flying. He holds her over his head. He settles her onto his shoulders as he begins to run across the lawn. There is a moment of mad excitement as he runs across the lawn with his baby. Bright flowers flash past him. Gold light is in his eyes. It is a kind of dance in which he shouts out ecstatic syllables that pass through him. He shouts out something obscene. The cries that come from him are not in a tongue he knows. They are in a language of the heart. The litte one, too, is crying out. The women are screaming, the dog is barking, but in his mad mood of exultation he takes the bark and all the screams for sounds of joy, for approbation, for applause. Their joy echoes his own. He runs and shouts and exults, at an immense distance from the women, from John, from the dog, from their shouting, the barking, their panic. Space has developed the capacity to expand. Everything that comes to him is unreal, as it was the first time he saw this place: the lawn, the jacarandas, and the oak tree. Yet he has never been so aware of his physical presence, of his legs running, the little one's weight on his shoulders, even his lips which are dry and chapped.

He runs toward the garages. The doors are open. He goes toward the silver Mercedes of his dreams. His wedding present, his. They have had it repaired just for him. It gleams as if new. It dazzles him with its top down, its black leather seats, its thick black knob of a gear shift. He has his spare keys in his pocket. He opens the car door and throws the little one into the back. He guns it out of the garage and down the driveway. He is aware of his hair on his scalp, of his sex, of his body soaring. He will fly now with the wind in his face. The jacarandas flash past. He leaves all order and rule and enters a place of primal savagery.

He looks over his shoulder. Kate runs across the lawn, drops her straw hat into the grass. She is running after him. She wants to come with him. The dog runs after her, too, barking loudly. The other children, Lydia's plait flying, follow. Kate runs down the driveway under the jacarandas after the

Mercedes. He catches a glimpse of the little one's white face in the back of the car. The bunches of her white hair swinging, she waves wildly, calling "*Kskatie! Kskatie!* Come with me."

Kate cries out to him to stop. She runs frantically over the gravel toward his car. She runs up behind his car, her light pink dress clinging to her body like water. He slows down and lets her catch up a little. She runs beside the car, her arms stretched out toward him. Her face is flushed and her eyes flash. Her mouth is wide. He stares at her familiar face, his wife's face, with sudden longing. He looks at his wife's pink dress, the sweat staining the armpits, the enamel bracelet on the slender wrist. He wants to take K.K. with him. He wants to do what he did before, in the night garden. He hears the clashing of wings. He remembers how he caught Marion up in his claws, and lifted her up. He carried her off through the air. There is no stopping him. He leaves himself behind. He will take K.K. along for the ride. He puts his foot on the brake. He comes to a halt. "Come with us, then," he says and grins at her and reaches across to open the door. She puts her hand on the door handle. She wants to be with him. All his blood is pumping. He is full with himself.

PART THREE

I

THE CHILD SCREAMS in the back of the car and beats on the leather for her to come with them. Kate stands with her hand on the hot metal handle. She doesn't want to look him in the eye. Turn you eyes away, she says to herself. Do not demean yourself by looking at a dog. But she cannot help it, she cannot remove her gaze from him. She cannot help looking into the yellow eyes, the sharp, exultant face.

She says, "Give me the child," but he shakes his head, the fair hair falling over his forehead, his arm stretched back over the back seat, containing the child. He laughs at Kate and invites her to join them, pushes open the door. She hesitates. He lunges forward and grabs her wrist. She feels his strong, bare hand scalding her flesh, the scandal of it, the strength. She can smell him, his odor of sweat and desire, and unaccountably her body feels heavy with fear and new excitement.

"Let's get out of here," he says, and for a moment she imagines the wild ride with him, the child falling safely asleep in her arms, the wind blowing on them. Would she discover what it was that drew her sister to him and robbed her of her will? Should she do what her sister did?

The garden starts to spin around her, and she fears she will faint, as she did as a girl. But this time she catches herself. What does she need him for now, anyway? What can he show her that she does not already know? Has she not gathered up all her sister has left behind, all that mattered, already? Is this any way to help the child?

She draws back, wrenches her arm free. He pulls the door shut and accelerates suddenly. When she tries to hold onto the handle, screams at him to give her the child, she is swept off her feet; she falls flat on the gravel on her knees and hands; she can still see Deidre's white face looking back at her, aghast.

She lies face-down on the gravel. Her knees and hands are bleeding, stones embedded in them. She drags herself up, runs back to the garage, and climbs into the Jaguar. The keys are dangling from the ignition, where Wilson has left them. She starts up the engine and speeds down the driveway, through the open gates. She looks right and left but sees nothing. She is uncertain which direction to take, cannot imagine where or why Louis would have taken the child off in this way. Had he stayed where he was, her mother would probably have let him remain. She drives frantically, fast, up and down the tree-lined streets of the neighborhood, looking for them. The streets seem emptier than usual, the Sunday silence a loud humming in her ears.

She curses her sister who should have told her more about this terrible man. Why had she not? But then had she ever really given her the chance? If she had listened to her sister rather than being so absorbed in her work, she might have realized what the situation was. The situation was clear to everyone who wanted to see.

What can he have been thinking? Should she have gone with him in the car? Why has he taken his little girl? To force them to let him back into the house? Will he telephone with demands, like a kidnapper?

She drives back to the clinic, sweating in the hot car, her sister's pink cotton dress sticking to her back, though she is almost certain he would not have gone back there. She stops the car, runs in and asks for the nurse, in her confusion forgetting that the nurse must be on her way to the house to fetch him.

When she arrives home, the children are sitting on the steps, waiting for her, holding onto the dog, their faces smudged with tears. John is not with them. "Where has John gone?" she asks, but they do not know.

II

HE WALKS ALONG THE ROAD in the glare of late afternoon light, unaware of the pale powder-dry dust of December, caught in the beams of light and streaming slantwise through the shade trees. The sun is about an hour above the horizon now, he can feel, before the swift coming of the summer night. He finds his way by habit. He knows this road, the one that leads into the city of Johannesburg, *eGoli.* On his afternoon off when he walks here, he hears the cars speeding by him and feels the fretwork of light and shade lifting and falling on his face and the hard pavement beneath his thin-soled shoes, smelling the odor of thick grass and gasoline. Sometimes, he rests by the side of the road with his gray hat tipped forward, shading his face under a tree, or he sits up, leaning against the bark smoking his pipe.

He's a good walker. He has walked for days on end during his life, striding on long, strong legs from one village to the next. He has always tried to avoid public transportation, such as it is: the crowded buses which never come on time and the trains which he knows are dangerous. But he is tired now, going along this road toward the city of gold in the twilight with the hot wind blowing against his body, making his khaki trousers flap against his thin legs. He knows he must hurry if he is to do what he must.

He knows this road, with the distinctive sounds of the different cars, just as he knows the different cries of the birds, the Indian mynas, who congregate in great clouds in one of the trees. He listens for the Mercedes and perhaps for the voice of the little one.

That one can scream for a long while and strongly. Not the kind to give up easily, his little one. He counts on her, but all he hears are the unfamiliar cars rushing past rudely, indifferently, dangerously, and a couple of dogs which gallop up and down a fence baying at him.

He walks on in the quickly gathering dusk, the light already a murky violet. The lamp lights have not yet been lit. He passes filling stations, shops, roadhouses, all closing up for the night. Sometimes when there is a break in the traffic, all he can hear is the swish of his khaki trouser legs rubbing together, and the wind sighing in the leaves. He is increasingly tired, and his muscles ache. His life, he thinks, is as light and insubstantial as a plume of smoke. He has little desire to hold onto it for much longer. It feels like too much effort for too little reward. He is thinking of all he has lost along the way: his first wife, the beloved one, whom he loved the most.

He remembers the white cloth fluttering from the pole on the top of the bride's *kraal* on the wedding day, the food at his wedding feast: the delicious buffalo meat; the well-cooked yams and corn cakes; the wild fowl, partridge and guinea; the baskets of wild figs and stewed *marulas* and the large fresh honey cakes. He remembers the dancing, the women like wands of fire, leaping and singing. He remembers the first real kiss on the mouth on the wedding night and crossing the threshold of the hut, the naked floor as smooth as silver. How beautiful she was, the bride of his youth, with her shiny, dark skin and her soft, plump body, adorned with the rings around her neck and ankles.

He remembers her gentle touch, the arms around his neck, the way she swung her hips, their nights together, nights of love and tenderness and laughter, lying together on the beaten earth floor of their hut in his *kraal*.

He still believes there is love in the world, brief moments of passion and long days of enduring affection. He still loves this young wife, as he loves his children who died so many years ago, all of them poisoned by an envious neighbor. He tries to imagine how anyone could hate him so much, how anyone could begrudge him the little he has. Envy, he knows, is a terrible and frightening force.

He has loved, too, these two white girl-children he has known from birth, though he believes the white man has failed his people. They have come to this country, raped and plundered and fought wars against his people, who have fought back and killed many white men. He knows about the place they called *Islandlwana*, where his people had killed so many of them. But the white man has won an unjust war with his weapons of fire which will one day destroy him, too. He has worked for them for many years, doing his duty with diligence and dignity, believing his people would be rewarded in the end. But there has been no reward; their lot has not improved. One day, he thinks, the Zulus will drive the white man back into the sea whence he came.

He keeps walking on through the hot December twilight, thinking of his warrior ancestors, who sang so beautifully before going into battle. He begins to sing a little, though he has never been much of a singer of songs, and he goes on almost despite himself, having once begun, mechanically, dragging himself forward despite the pain in his legs and his feet and the last glare of the sinking sun.

He knows where he is heading, and what he must do when he arrives. But he is afraid now that his pace is too slow, that he will arrive too late. It is further than he had imagined. It is always further than one imagines in life. Every journey is longer and harder than it seemed at the start. And yet one has to keep walking. He thinks how he has kept polishing the floors and the silver and the shoes, even the soles of the shoes.

He thinks the place where he is going will be shut up by the time he arrives, or if not, he may not be allowed to enter, an old black man, a Zulu, anonymous, even to his own kind, forgotten even by his own children, part of a vanished world.

III

H E TURNS ON THE RADIO and finds loud music. He turns up the volume. He tries to talk the child into singing along, the way they used to do. But she has started up her whimpering. She whimpers softly, her face turned into the leather seat. Once they are on the highway, in the fast lane, she starts to scream.

"Cut that out," he says. "I can't drive if you scream like that." But she continues.

He is trapped in the heat of the car and the thick traffic. He no longer flies. His lungs are filled with the fumes from the exhaust. He hadn't thought of that. He hadn't thought of anything. Rush hour. Of course. He cannot move. He has come down to earth with a jolt. All his life he has felt these extreme shifts of mood. He looks in the rear-view mirror to make sure that no one is following him. The little one refuses even to look at him.

His shirt sticks to his back. Perspiration trickles down his forehead and his legs. He is weighted down, heavy. The child keeps screaming all the way along the road, hesitating only to take in a big shuddering breath in order to start up again. It is embarrassing. People are staring. He is obliged to turn and lash out at her blindly with the back of his hand. Enough to drive you mad.

And she smells. He glances back at her. He groans. "Goddamn it!" he shouts. He sees that she has peed in her pants, staining his leather seats. Infuriatingly, she kicks her legs against the back seat. Bloody kid. She's beginning to get on his nerves in a serious way.

He wonders what is going on at Crossways. He wonders if the Kempdens will have called the police. There is no reason for them to, but he suspects K.K. might have. It is the sort of thing she would do. He has done nothing wrong, after all. He feels a little rush of defiance come over him. He begins to find arguments in his own defense. His intention was a good one. He simply wanted to be on his own with his child. K.K. wanted to send him back to the hospital. It is her fault. If K.K. had not been there, the old ladies would have let him do what he wanted. All they want is peace and quiet; they would have been glad to have the child off their hands. He just wanted to take her for a little drive and a swim, in this heat, as he has done so many times before. He had even offered to take K.K. with them, but she declined. He hasn't thought much further than that, just as he hadn't really thought of what he would do that night coming back from the party with his wife.

His wife, incredibly, had thought fit to read his letter. Not only had she read it, but she insisted on doing something about it.

He would never have imagined her capable of doing something like that. He had never thought that there was anything she would not condone. His polite and well-brought-up and oh-so-Christian Marion: always turning the other cheek. She loved turning the other bloody cheek. Always rushing off to church to pray away any aggression or to get inspiration for doing good deeds. But she had read a letter not addressed to her. She had insisted he clear up the matter. She had stolen his money. She had taken a lover—two fucking lovers. She had deceived him. She threatened to leave him if he did not clear up the matter. Well, she had got her wish.

IV

T HE SILVER TRAY WITH THE DRINKS has been brought in as usual.
The cut-glass beakers and the decanters chink, as the
maid carries the tray to the table between the French windows.
There are the silver bowl of yellow and white freesias, and the
small, starched white napkins. The glasses are filled, the olives
and the nuts are offered, but no one eats. Her mother sits on
the sofa, sipping the whiskey in her glass, her hands shaking.
Her aunt sits on her right, bolt upright, making sure her sister
takes her pills to keep her quiet through this terrible night.

Her mother looks up at the young maid and asks in a
despairing voice, "Where is John? Why is he not serving my
drink tonight? He always serves it."

The maid says she supposes he must have gone to look for
the baby. She saw him walking off down the driveway.

"Don't tell me he's gone and disappeared, too? Why isn't he
here when I need him? What have I done to deserve this?"

The young maid removes the nuts. She passes the olives
around again.

Kate sits at the other end of the sofa with the children on
either side. For once, they have been allowed to sit with the

grown-ups and share the nuts and olives, and even drink a Coca-Cola, but they take nothing, and no one encourages them to.

Finally, Kate can bear it no longer, so she crumples her spotless white napkin in her hand and rises from the sofa and says, since it is after six o'clock and Louis is not back, she is going to call the police.

Her aunt puts her drink down and says, "And what will you tell them? That the father has taken his daughter for a ride?"

Her mother murmurs, "What can they do, darling?"

She shouts, "They can find him, that's what they can do! They can find Deidre!"

Lydia, who still wears her red dress and her long white socks, but has lost the red ribbon in her hair, opens up her mouth and wails, "I want my sister!" Kate would like to do the same thing, to weep for her own sister. She feels she has failed her again. She has not protected her children as she should have done. She has allowed her youngest child to be carried off. Who knows what might have happened to her by now?

She tells the maid to take the children up for their bath, that they are exhausted and weeping. She tells her mother to go to bed, too, and watches her climb the stairs with her aunt following. She goes to the black phone in the hall and calls the emergency number. Then she waits for the police to arrive in the lounge.

V

HE HEARS THE SOUND OF A LORRY and the cries of his kind, who are hanging onto the back. He lifts his thumb and calls out in Zulu to ask for a lift. He, too, will hang onto the back. He can do that, surely. But the day laborers laugh at him and tell him he will fall off and break his old back, and the lorry sweeps by him, blowing dust into his eyes. He shakes his fist at them, at such insolence, or is it only indifference, the indifference of the young?

To his surprise, he becomes aware that another car has stopped beside him, and that a man is asking courteously in Zulu if he needs to go somewhere. He can only discern the dark cap and the hand which beckons, for his world is falling asunder now, and it is slipping from him.

He thanks the driver for his courtesy, is asked to get in then, he will be taken where he needs to go. He hesitates, not quite certain the driver is real and not a figment of his imagination, a response to his desire for rest. Black men don't usually drive cars around here. Perhaps this man is a spirit, a ghost, or even the *Tokolosh* in disguise, come to taunt him, to collect him and take him to the land of the dead. Or perhaps it is the spirit of one of his warrior ancestors come to his rescue? When he realizes it is only a black taxi driver, he says he has no money to pay for his ride.

"Get in, *baba*, I'll take you where you need to go for free. What is an old blind man doing shuffling along the road at this hour of night?" the driver asks him rudely.

But he gets in and asks him to speak politely. He tells him who his ancestors are, and where he comes from, and where he needs to go.

"That place will be shut up, and besides they won't let a black man with no money in there, whoever his ancestors were. Surely you know that."

He says nothing, but repeats that that is where he has to go and that this man is not to waste his time, if he doesn't want to take him there.

The driver laughs and says he sees he is a stubborn old man, but he'll take him there. He looks like his father, who died recently in the homeland, he says, somewhat tactlessly, John thinks.

"I'm not dead yet," he says.

The man chuckles, slaps his knee, and takes off fast and aggressively through the traffic. At any other moment John would have told him not to waste his petrol driving so fast, and to be more careful, but now he says nothing. He is not in a position to complain. He is in a hurry.

The driver takes him right up to the big, high gates.

"You have a home to go to, *baba*, and is it far from here?" the driver asks him impudently.

Of course, he has a home, he says with great dignity. It is a home in one of the best suburbs of Johannesburg, and he mentions the name of the house, built by a famous architect, though he suspects the driver does not know the names of architects. The house is on a most elegant street, and he tells him its name, too, and even gives the number of the house. He works for fine people, who live in a fine house, he assures the driver, a mansion with many rooms and much fine furniture and fine silver. He does not work for the kind of white riffraff he sees around these days. He wants to tell the driver that he has always had a good place to go to, because he has always worked hard and honestly, unlike the driver who makes an easy living in a white man's machine.

The driver says that if he wishes to enter into this place, though he can see no reason why he would want to, all he needs to do is to slip through the fence, through the hole over there, and the driver indicates something with an arm.

He thanks him, nods, and climbs down, saluting, and tells him he may have saved a life, though not John's own. He runs his hand along the fence searching for the hole.

VI

H E DRIVES THE SILVER MERCEDES into the parking lot, as he has done so many times before, though this is not at all like those.

He lifts the screaming child from the back seat. Her pants, her dress, even her socks are soaked with urine. He tells her he is taking her swimming, as they did before on Sundays. "Don't you want to go swimming with Daddy?" he asks, shaking his head at her in wonderment. She continues to scream bloody murder. She screams for her brother and sister, for her *Kskatie,* even for her goddamn grandmother. She even screams for her dead "Mormie." She bangs her fists against his shoulder and face. One strikes his nose, causing pain. He slaps her back hard across the cheek. People turn to stare at him, as he carries her through the cars in the stale heat of the late afternoon.

This is not what he has imagined, lying in his hospital bed. He had imagined his children, his gold-headed angels, rushing to him and climbing lovingly on his lap. They should have clung to him with shouts of jubilation, and not looked at him as if they didn't even recognize him, staring at him in silence with fear in their eyes.

His baby, his favorite one, the one who resembles him most, continues to scream and cry for her "Mormie." She has let him down. She has disappointed him. He should have taken these children with their mother in the car, as he had planned, that night, after all. What is left for them in their lives now, anyway?

His children, he realizes, as he wanders through the cars in the parking lot, holding his screaming baby in his arms, have forgotten him completely. It has only taken them three months to forget their father, while he has lain helplessly in his hospital bed. He can see he means nothing to them now. His wife's sister has turned them against him. He doesn't know what she has told them, but it must have been a pack of lies.

Sweating in the heat, he carries the squirming child with difficulty. He pins her arms, so that she cannot hit him. She doesn't resemble the white-headed baby of his dreams now. She certainly doesn't look like him any more. Her mouth has grown into a great red gash in her face, like her screaming aunt's, like his mother's. Her eyes are smaller, slyly slanted, and dark. They look almost oriental. Where did she get eyes like that? The red nose is running with snot, like a little black piccanin on the farm. She has lost the absurd elastics they had put in her hair, and it falls into her face like straw. He has the impression now that this is not his child at all, but rather someone else's, a little devil. Where has she come from? What if he were not the father of this child? How does he really know for certain she is his, knowing what he knows about his wife who has betrayed him?

He puts her down on the hot, tarred road. He takes a hard swipe at her bottom. He tells her to shut up. *"Hou jou bek,"* he says. This makes her scream even louder. She stamps her foot at him in her patent-leather shoe and her white sock, furious.

They have spoiled her completely, he can see. They have ruined his child, if she is his. Obviously she has had no discipline at all. No child of his would react like this. He is tempted to leave her screaming at his feet on the pavement. The sun is setting, but the air is still hot. There is no wind. It is later than he had thought. There are people all around him, watching curiously. He doesn't need this trouble in a public place. He goes up to the gate, dragging the child by the arm. He fumbles for his wallet. Does he have any money? He hadn't thought of money. He holds onto the child's arm with one hand, dangling her like a rag doll.

The guard tells him the place is closing up in less than an hour. He can enter without paying the fee, if he wishes. "Go on, go on. Hurry, if you want to get a swim," he says in Afrikaans and waves him through the gate. He is probably glad to get rid of him, and the screaming, stinking child. Everyone seems to be leaving. He wants to reach out to them and tell them to stay. He remembers friendly faces, compliments.

A woman wearing a green turban and red lipstick stops and says, indignantly, "That must hurt her shoulder." He glares back at her, telling her to mind her own bloody business. He considers taking a swipe at her red mouth, too. He's in no mood to take that kind of lip. Then he notices the strapping husband standing belligerently beside her. He softens, smiles, raises his eyebrows, and says, "*Kinders!*" The couple stare back at him for a moment but then just shake their heads and go on their way.

He lifts the child up onto his shoulders and makes his way through the crowd of people who are beginning to leave the pool. They turn their heads to stare at the screaming child, who is beating her feet against his chest and drumming her fists on the top of his head. He goes along the edge of the pool toward the concrete changing rooms in a hurry now, almost banging her head on the door jamb. "Watch out!" a man shouts over his shoulder, passing them.

VII

S HE OPENS THE DOOR for the policemen when they arrive and wonders if they were the same ones who came to knock on the door late at night to announce her sister's death to John. She asks them to sit down in the lounge, but they remain standing by the windows, with the curtains drawn on the night.

She makes an attempt to explain the situation as succinctly as she can. She is conscious, as she speaks, of the minutes passing and is aware of what could be happening elsewhere. They do not seem to understand what she is saying.

"The father has taken his little girl for a ride in his car?" the taller one says, pushing his cap back and scratching his head, looking puzzled.

"Not quite right in the head, you say? A medical doctor? Now why is that?" the other one asks. She notices a finger missing on one of his hands.

"You are the aunt, is that right? Domiciled in France? And where is the mother then?" the first one asks, peering at her, as if this living abroad in France might constitute something illegal, as if she were the one under suspicion.

Surely it is enough that her sister should have been killed, Kate thinks, without this also happening? Why does she have to go through this again?

"And you have no idea where he might have gone with the little girl?" the other one says.

She shakes her head, tears of exasperation welling up in her eyes. "That's why I have called you!" she exclaims and knocks her fist against her forehead. And these are the men who run this country! She recalls stories about the stupidity of the South African police and how they were supposed to have banned the book *Black Beauty* for its title. She wonders now if she should have called the accountant's detective instead of these incompetents. Perhaps she should have followed his advice. Why had she not made a decision before this happened? How indecisive she has been in her life, never confronting anything, always running away. What is the matter with her?

"We are trying to help you, Miss," the taller one says with some dignity. "That's why we are asking these questions. It's the only way we can help you." It seems to her that the man smells slightly of alcohol as well as, strongly, of tobacco.

The questions go on and on, infuriatingly, round and round. The first one writes something down in a notebook, looks around the room, and walks out the French doors into the garden for a moment, though the sky is quite black now, starless, and there is nothing to be seen or heard out there except the monotonous keening of the crickets. When he returns, he tracks mud onto the carpet with his thick-soled shoes, and she thinks John will be upset. And where is he? How could he have disappeared at such a moment? Why is she having to handle this alone?

"I suggest that you keep calm and wait until morning, and if the little girl is not back by then, we will begin a serious search. In all probability the father will bring his child back on his own, or he will telephone you. There is no reason for him not to, is there? Strictly speaking, there is nothing we can do. She is, after all, his own child, if we have understood rightly, Miss, and he has never lost custody, if I understand correctly. He can take her wherever he wishes. The doctors in the hospital seem to have felt there was no danger in this visit. Surely they would know? Medical men, after all, hey?"

"Please," she says in desperation, "you have to find them. There is no telling what he will do."

The men stare blankly at her.

She is obliged to put it bluntly; there is no other way. "This man has killed his wife, he has murdered my sister. He beat his children unconscious, their bodies are covered with welts. Who knows what he will do now, desperate as he is to get his life back, to pretend that nothing has happened? He could do anything to his child, whether he plans to or not, on an impulse." As she says the words aloud she realizes that they are true, that there is no disputing them, and she begins to shake.

But the policemen look at her as if she is overdramatizing the situation, exaggerating, and talking herself into a state. Obviously they don't believe a word. Why should they, she thinks. She is practically a foreigner, and she is accusing a well-known surgeon, an upstanding member of the community. They leave her alone to her own devices.

She stands for a moment trying to think what to do. She thinks of Rene, her life in France, her work. Then she strides fast across the lawn, going to the servants' quarters to see if John has come back. Surely he will be able to help. But the door to his room is open and the room, empty. She opens a door to one of the other rooms. She finds the maid, who is pulling her dress over her head. She catches a glimpse of her strong, bare back. She apologizes and asks if she has any idea where John might have gone to look for the little one. Would she have any idea? The maid looks at her with frightened eyes and tells her she has just remembered what she should have said before, that he told her he was going to the public pool, the one where the *baas* used to go on Sundays with the children.

She goes back to the hall, picks up her handbag, the car keys. She runs back outside across the lawn to the garage and climbs into the Jaguar and switches on the headlights. She turns on the radio, finds some music, and turns up the volume. She drives down the driveway under the jacarandas. She feels almost happy for a moment to be going somewhere definite. She remembers driving Rene's old beat-up Citroën very fast through the hills of Provence. She is often the one who drives, while he talks and waves his hands. He is not a good driver.

She is making a decision at last. She has fumbled and muddled for too long. She has to find the little one. Perhaps John will have already come upon them. He will need her help.

VIII

H E GOES BACK TO THE GATE and almost trips over an iron shovel lying on the ground. He lifts it easily over his shoulder. The guard is sitting by the gate in a deck chair and appears to be dozing, as far as John can see. He walks up to the turnstyle, and is about to slip through, when he hears the guard whistle and call out to him. "Hey there! Where you think you are going! There is an entrance fee," he calls out rudely. He is cleaning his nails with a penknife and glancing up at John impudently.

John mumbles something about the pipes, about having to dig a hole to get at a broken pipe.

The guard says, "You are not allowed in here." John adds some words in Zulu, telling the man to leave him alone. "*Ngiyeke*," he says. He often does this, as none of them speak his language. In English he says, "Burst pipes, emergency. Work to do." The guard shrugs his shoulders and says, "All right, go on then, do your work," and lets him shuffle through.

He has never been to the public pool, where the swimming competitions and the tennis matches are held. He knows this is where Miss Marion and *Kskatie* would come to practice swimming and diving, and where they would swim in the big competitions and win all the prizes they would bring home. He knows this is where the *baas* would take the children on Sundays with the picnic John packed for them with the chicken in the basket and the cold Coca-Colas and bottle opener and the paper napkins that he never forgot to pack, neatly.

The children would tell him about the big pool, about the many other children there and the noise, when they came back with their skin sunburned, noses peeling, exhausted. He could not imagine why the *baas* wanted to take them to such a noisy, packed public pool, where the children must do heaven-knows-what in the water, when they could just as well have stayed home by their own quiet, clean pool, which he made sure was kept clean, and reminded the poolboy to put the chlorine in every day in the right dosage.

They must take him for a workman, a poolman himself, for no one tells him that he has no right to be here. He wanders on in the shadows with the big iron shovel over his shoulder, blindly, shuffling his way towards the smell of chlorine and the cries of the last few bathers remaining in the pool, he surmises.

He is listening for the sound of a child crying. Perhaps he was mistaken after all, and the *baas* has taken the little girl somewhere else. There are hundreds of places where he might have gone, after all. Perhaps he was frightened and just kept driving. But he does not believe that; he believes people are like himself, and do the same things over and over again, as he has done in his life. They do again what they have done before, returning to the same places, treading the same ground, round and round, like a jackal returning to a familiar place to die.

The sun has already set, as he can feel by the coolness in the air. There are few people about now, no more voices. Perhaps they have already come and gone back to the house in their fast car, while he was walking along the road. If only his eyes were not so feeble and his legs! He has been lucky with his health over the years, he knows, but he feels he does not have the strength to walk all the way home, so he stands there, breathing heavily.

He is very tired now. He wants only to lie down and sleep, and he is not quite sure where to go. He feels confused, in this strange place. He shuffles across the grass, lifting his head, listening. Why does he not hear anything from the child? What has happened to her? Without sound, he is indeed lost. He does not like this silence; it seems sinister to him. It reminds him of returning to his kraal after his wife and children had died and the desolate silence he found there. He goes through a door into what he supposes must be the changing rooms, a labyrinth of dark passageways and small cubicles—showers and lavatories perhaps. He blunders about, pushing doors open, staring blindly inside.

He can smell the damp in here and the odor of chlorine and of mold. He had hoped to recognize the child's cries. He gets confused and turns around and retraces his steps, going doggedly from door to door. The floor is wet and slippery, and he is afraid of falling. He clutches the iron spade with one hand and feels his way along the wall with the other. He traces the stipled walls with the tips of his fingers.

He feels as if he has done this before in some other life, or in a dream, blundering around in the half-dark, looking for a lost child in a maze. He thinks of his dead children, his beautiful dead wife, and how easily they were taken from him. He shivers and his old bones ache. How fragile we are, how easily we slip from life, he thinks. Someone he nearly stumbles over cries out, "Bloody kaffir!" from a blur of abundant white flesh.

IX

THE CHANGING ROOMS ARE ALMOST EMPTY. He hears a guard calling out to clear the rooms. It is closing time. He pays no attention to that. He carries the child with her face pressed against his chest, his hand slipped over her mouth to keep her quiet. He walks fast down the dimly lit corridor with its smells of chlorine and mold. With his elbow, he opens the door to one of the rooms at the very end of the passageway. He drops the child down on the wooden bench. The back of her head bangs hard against the concrete wall and then falls forward. She slumps there, silent, finally, head on her chest. Her white hair hangs in her face. Her pink legs dangle. She has somehow lost her shoes and even the long socks. Her feet are bare. Someone else's child, hardly a child. She looks unreal to him, a stuffed doll in a rumpled pink dress.

Perhaps, had she behaved, he would simply have taken her back to the house. Now he's not sure that would be wise. He glances at her, slumped over on the bench. He has only taken what is rightfully his, after all.

He leaves her there and closes the door behind him. He wanders out to the empty pool and the setting sun.

He stands for a moment looking around uncertainly. The place seems altered, shadowy. The familiar place is strange to him now. He hardly recognizes it. He remembers sparkling water, well-marked swimming lanes, fast swimmers. The long pool looks murky in the evening light. The water looks dark and cold. He thinks he sees slime on the walls. A lone swimmer seems to be floating on his back and staring up at the darkening sky.

He stands at the edge of the pool and stares at the water. He notices a black bathing cap lying on the tiles at the side of the pool, and he picks it up, feels the worn plastic give way in his hands, discards it.

A strange sleepiness has come over him, a torpor of the mind. He has no longer any desire to take his child swimming. He knows she is in no condition to swim, nor is he. The whole idea of swimming seems absurd.

Everything seems suspended for a last moment between day and night, as M.K. would do for a moment in the air when she dived, hovering in an extended arc outside the life of day. His body, too, is suspended in the stillness, the suspension of all activity, a perpetual blue-gray gloom.

He had put his wife up on a pedestal, and then she had disappointed him. He had thought the world of her. He had imagined they would always be together. He had thought they could help one another in times of trouble. He had thought he could go to her, and she would understand that no one else meant anything to him. He had imagined that others seeing them together would have envied their obvious closeness as he had envied her closeness with her sister. He had counted on her absolutely. But she had not understood him. She never spoke his language properly.

She had behaved like a slut. She had gone off with her Turk. Then she had run off with that weasel of an accountant. She had read a letter, not addressed to her. She had insisted that he explain it, that he go and see that woman, when it was obvious that would not have helped. Then she had threatened to leave him. He would have been exposed, his career ruined.

It was easy to slip something into her glass at the party. It was easy to get his wife to drink more; she liked it. He helped her to the car. She waved good-bye to her friends. She even managed to remove a stone from her shoe. A silver pole at the side of the road caught his headlights, and he drove straight into it. He had intended to kill himself as well. At the last minute he must have turned the wheel away.

Now he stands in the dim light at the edge of the pool. The place is very quiet. The crowd has all gone. They have left him alone, here. He hears a few guards wandering around, locking up. It is the loneliest place in the world, he thinks. The water shimmers pinkish-gray in the twilight. What has happened to his life? What remains for him now?

He sees the sisters as they were long ago, in their dusky skins, the dark hair down their backs. They swim through the water with their arms and legs entwined. They are going under together and then coming up, spitting out water and giggling. He feels as far from them as he ever did, far from everyone else as well. He is spinning. The whole world spins around him, a vast moving screen of orange-and-pink light. The long pool with its divided lanes shimmers and invites him in.

He wanders along its edge. He leans up against the trunk of a jacaranda. He looks up into the branches, the light feathery leaves, the violet sky. He remembers that evening in the garden with Serge when his wife had come upon them. Serge has not come to visit him in the hospital. Has he, too, betrayed him in the end?

X

S HE DRIVES FAST IN THE DARK toward the public pool, the
window open and the hot night wind on her face. The
wind has blown the cloud cover from the sky, and the stars
and moon are visible. She has always liked the night. She
remembers how she would call herself Moon and her sister
Sun. Once, her sister had danced the sun dance on the school
lawn and lost her yellow petticoat.

She is still in her sister's summer dress, and it sticks to her
back like a second skin. Her mouth is dry and her eyes ache.

The traffic flows easily now, and she weaves in and out.
She thinks of the mechanic telling her mother that the car was
having problems because no one ever drove it fast enough. Her
mother permitted herself so few pleasures now.

She looks right and left, staring out the window in hopes of
seeing any of them or even the car. Perhaps she will see Louis
going in the opposite direction. Perhaps the police were right
to suggest that she was exaggerating. She wonders if the pool
is closed by now. Surely he will tire of the little one and bring
her home. She worries about John out there, too, wandering
around blindly somewhere, looking for the child.

XI

H E OPENS A DOOR and sees the little one slumped on the bench. He picks her up and cradles her in his arms and walks outside. Her head is thrown back over his arm, her mouth agape, and her white-blond hair hangs down, swinging back and forth. She seems to be sleeping.

As he emerges from the maze of changing rooms, the sky is dark. He looks up for a moment, but through his dim eyes he does not see the *baas* walking out the gate.

XII

S HE IS NOT SURE OF THE WAY and drives around the pool area through the narrow, shadowy streets. She drives on toward death in the gathering dark.

She sees a group of vendors milling around a brazier, their faces illuminated fleetingly by the flickering light. They are packing up their wares. A thin man carries a large sack on his back. A woman with a *doek* around her head picks up something he has dropped behind him on the ground.

Kate can smell the polluted air, the gasoline, and night fires. She turns down the radio, slows down to ask the vendors where the entrance to the public pool is found. A large woman approaches, carrying a box of pineapples. She grins at Kate toothlessly and peddles her wares, lifting up the cardboard box with the pineapples to the window to show Kate. Kate can see, even in the dim light, that they are rotting. The woman insists, lowering her price. Kate waves her away impatiently, asking the man, with a woolen cap over his head, the way.

When she arrives at the gate to the pool, she finds to her dismay, that it is shut, and the guard about to leave. She stops the car by the gate. She jumps out leaving the lights on, the keys in the ignition, her handbag on the seat. She asks the guard if he has seen a crying child with a blond man. He shakes his head at her question, shrugs his shoulders impatiently and says he has seen a million crying children with a million blond men.

"Perhaps you have seen a tall black man with a child in a pink dress and patent-leather shoes?" she tries again.

He shakes his head at her. How could he remember such a thing? He glances at her rudely, in a hurry to get home she can see. What is she going to do now? Where should she go? Where can they be? She gets back into her car and drives aimlessly through the streets.

Then she sees a man walking down the side of a narrow street. In the light of the street lamp she recognizes his familiar long-legged walk, the khaki trousers, the narrow, high head. She realizes with a lift of her heart that he has something pale and glimmering in his arms, and he is staggering under its weight. He staggers, zigzagging back and forth on the pavement. She swerves to the side of the road, and the car behind her honks loudly.

She leans across the seat, puts her head out of the window, and calls out to him. He stops, looks up, and stumbles toward her under the light of the streetlamp. She throws open the car door and tells him to get in.

He climbs in beside her and sits there slumped, unmoving, head on his chest. He seems almost asleep with his sleeping burden.

She leans over and peers at the child's face. In the ghostly green light of the dashboard, her white-gold head seems framed as if with a halo. Her round smooth face is tilted upwards on John's arm, the half-open eyes seem to be dreaming, the skin pink and white, the plum-dark mouth slightly open as if in song. The little one looks to her like one of Fra Angelico's angels.

"Is she alright?" she asks him, reaching over to take the child into her arms. But he clings onto her.

She looks down at Deidre and says her name, but the child does not respond. Kate reaches for the small fingers and toes and finds them cold. She trembles, her knees watery with fear. She brushes the white hair back from the forehead with the tips of her fingers.

"What has happened?" she asks, and he takes her hand in his hard callused one and guides it to the back of the child's head. She feels the knob, as big as an egg. She says, "She's hurt. Is she breathing?" and he nods his head.

"She will be alright, only a little death," he says.

She slips her hand under the rumpled pink dress with its embroidered rosebuds, that the child had asked to wear earlier that day for her daddy's visit because it was the same color as Kate's. She feels under the drawstring vest. She lays her hand on the child's heart and feels the warm, damp flesh and the almost imperceptible rise and fall. She leans down and puts her cheek near the child's mouth and feels the warm breath.

She weeps with her hands to her face. She says she should never, never have come out here. She has caused nothing but trouble. Look at what has occurred. Without John's help she would never even have found the child.

He shakes his head and murmurs that he is glad she came back. She remembers him standing at the gate to greet her, his head tilted, calling her *inkosazana*, then lifting her up in the air and onto his back, carrying her through the shadows and the light of the garden. She remembers coming into the kitchen to show him her first white dance dress, with the full skirt and the tight waist. She remembers him looking her over carefully and then nodding his head in grave approbation. She recalls coming down the corridor once, carelessly naked, when she had forgotten her soap, and his turning his eyes toward the ceiling with horror, so as not to see her young body. She sees him getting down onto his knees in the bathroom when she was ill and wiping up her vomit from the tile floor. She sees him carrying her mother over his shoulder, carefully, up the stairs to her bed. He has been carrying her and her kind for too long.

Then she sees a familiar figure coming down the street toward the car, the white hair falling low over the forehead, the jut of the chin, the high safari collar, the smart shoes. She hears the tap-tap of the quick steps on the pavement.

XIII

H E WALKS FAST NOW in the night air. He is not going any
distance and has no need for his car. For once he prefers
to walk. He sees the moon and the stars, and he peers ahead
into the bramble of trees and shrubs on one side of the road,
checking the edge of smoky darkness. He feels he is in a sort
of antechamber. He is at the furthest point from where he
started. His body is leaving the earth again. He is filled with his
old sense of power. The night wind has lifted him and carried
him away. He walks a few inches above the pavement, in air.
He is no longer sure what he is doing on this narrow, mean
street. The women, men, and boys he has slept with, all seem
one to him. He cannot tell them apart.

He hears a rustling in the bushes. A young girl walks by
him, saying to the man at her side, "Oh, no, no you don't! Not
that," and laughs.

He is swept along by an outside force. He goes toward
Serge's flat, though he has no intention of seeing him. He
wonders how long this feeling of omnipotence will last.

Then he notices a black car parked on the other side of the
road in the light of the streetlamp. He recognizes it as his

mother-in-law's. Someone must have come looking for him. They have come after him with evil intent, that is clear. They haven't sent the police, but they have come, themselves, to find him. They have come to lock him up. With a shock of surprise, he sees Kate sitting in the driver's seat with John beside her, the child in his arms. He goes on walking fast toward them. He has known from the start that this sister means trouble. He will deal with her before she causes him any more of it. He should have done this when he had the chance.

Then he hears her start up the car. He hears the familiar muffled roar. The headlights come on smartly and disclose him. Music is immediately blaring from within. He sees her face, lit up with the green light of the dashboard. She looks almost ghostly to him, her eyes large and hollow. He can see her fingers on top of the leather steering wheel. He hears the surge of the engine.

XIV

S HE STARTS UP FAST toward the familiar figure. There is nothing but the moon, the stars, and the music blaring, with, in the distance, the low sound of the traffic and the hot wind. It occurs to her that she could simply drive past the man, but what would happen then? What further violence would follow? The thick stars throb in the darkness of the night and call out to her. She can feel the sweat trickle down her forehead, as it did at her sister's funeral. Her face is burning. She hears her sister's voice calling her.

Look at her. She sees her sister coming to her through the dark, drawing her onwards. She feels her sister's presence standing before her as she stood before her in the street, saying good-bye. She sees her sleeves flapping in the wind. She feels her soft arms around her neck. She sees her dead sister, her lost childhood, her lost dreams. Her sister is part of her.

She goes toward him, and he does not step out of the headlights of her car. He is caught in the lights like a trapped deer. She can see the glimmer of his white face, and he seems to be laughing at her. He is running toward her, laughing. What does he want from her now? What harm does he intend? Does he think he will persuade her, this time, to come with him? Does he think that this one will do just as well as the other, that she will be a suitable replacement for the one who let him down?

She sees it all clearly now, as she drives straight for him. She does not swerve. The big car strikes him with a heavy jolt, but she hardly feels it. John is clutching the child's face to his breast.

She drives on. Neither of them looks back. She hears a car going the other way stop with a screech of brakes, a shout.

She comes to a halt under a tree in a street that leads to the hospital. She is shaking with the beating of her heart. She turns off the music, the lights.

He says, as he had long before, "Perhaps it is better like this." He tells her that it is urgent for her to get to the airport now. It would be better for her not to remain in this place any longer.

He tells her he will stay on with the children. She must drive him to the hospital and leave him and the child and the car there. He will telephone her mother. They will send on her things.

"I will tell them all the old stories," he promises her, as the child leans her head against his chest.

"*Lala sithandwa, lal' uphumule,*" he says. Sleep beloved one, sleep and rest.